THE DEVIL SNAR'D

THE DEVIL SNAR'D

GEORGE R. PREEDY

With an introduction by

Gina R. Collia

NEZU
PRESS

Published by Nezu Press
Queensgate House,
48 Queen Street,
Exeter, Devon,
EX4 3SR,
United Kingdom.

This edition published 2023
Editorial material and introduction © Gina R. Collia 2023
The Devil Snar'd first published by Ernest Benn Ltd., 1932.

ISBN-13: 978-1-7393921-1-6

Opposite: 'Miss Marjorie Bowen', Dover Street Studios,
taken from *The Bystander,* 5 September 1906, p. 41.

'I have used many names for business purposes, but they were none of them of my choosing and seemed rather to be fastened on me like a series of masks.' - Margaret Campbell, *Myself When Young: By Famous Women of Today*, 1938.

Best known as Marjorie Bowen, Margaret Gabrielle Vere Campbell wrote under several other names: Joseph Shearing, Robert Paye, John Winch and George R. Preedy, the latter being used for the present title.

The Many Masks of Margaret Campbell
by Gina R. Collia

Margaret Gabrielle Vere Campbell was born into poverty in a seaside cottage on Hayling Island, east of Portsmouth in Hampshire, on 1 November 1885.[1] She was the second child of Vere Douglas Campbell (1853–1906) and Josephine Elizabeth Campbell (née Ellis, 1860–1921). Her father, an alcoholic who disappeared from her life almost entirely by the time she was five years old, was always kind to her, but she was never close to her mother, who was prone to 'hysterical ill-humour',[2] scolded her frequently and repeatedly told her 'You ought never to have been born.'[3]

Margaret received no formal education as a child. Her mother, an aspiring writer and playwright, attempted to teach her to read and write, but this simply increased her annoyance towards her daughter; five-year-old Margaret was frequently slapped on the back of the hands with a hair-brush or shut in a room without food as a punishment for 'refusing to spell out of obstinacy.'[4] Nana, the housekeeper, eventually succeeded where her mother had failed, but Margaret had little access to books at that time. Her family moved from one lodging house to another, to avoid settling debts, and she made use of whatever she could find to read on the current landlady's bookshelf.

When the family moved to Kensington, Margaret began to educate herself with books borrowed from the local library, and when, having been evicted for non-payment of rent, they moved again to lodgings on Vauxhall Bridge Road, she began visiting the National Gallery, the British Museum and the South Kensington

Museums. At the time she dreamed of becoming a great artist, and one of her mother's friends suggested that her passion for art should be encouraged, as there might be money in it. She applied to attend the Royal College of Arts in South Kensington, but she failed the entrance examination. Then, after several more moves to new lodgings to avoid paying yet more creditors, her mother decided that she should attend the Slade School of Fine Art, which she did from 1901 to 1904. But her work was regarded as poor by her professors, she failed both of the examinations she took whilst there, she was perpetually embarrassed by her mother's failure to pay her tuition fees on time, and she 'began to be aware of the disability of sex'.[5] As a result, she lived in a 'constant state of depression and terror.'[6] She went without food on a daily basis, was embarrassed by the state of her poor clothing, and she felt that every other student was a better artist than she was. Deflated and despairing, she turned to writing and, as there was no money to buy paper, took to scribbling out stories and notes on the backs of her own drawings.

When Margaret was about fourteen or fifteen years old, and following several more house moves, the family took lodgings in a street off Russell Square, and she managed to get some work carrying out research and fact-checking in the British Museum. By that time, she had nearly finished writing a novel and had completed a number of poems and short stories, but her mother, who had failed to secure any interest in her own writing, attempted to persuade her against pursuing a literary career. In an attempt to force her to focus on her painting and drawing, she sent Margaret to Paris, but she failed to provide enough money to pay for lodgings, let alone tuition costs for art school classes. Despite her circumstances—'I was hungrier then than I had ever been'[7]—Margaret enjoyed her time in Paris, visiting museums and galleries and adding to her knowledge of art and history, but she made no progress in her career as an artist and returned to writing.

When she had been in Paris almost a year, Margaret's mother sent for her to return home. Once back in London, she showed some of her writing to her mother; Mrs Campbell's response was to declare it 'hopeless'.[8] This did not, however, prevent her from sending her young daughter's novel, the swashbuckling historical romance *The Viper of Milan*, to an agent. His response was not encouraging: the story was not believable, he disliked the unhappy ending, and it was 'not the kind of thing… that a girl was expected to write.'[9] The novel went on to be rejected by eleven publishers, and Mrs Campbell suggested that her daughter find an alternative way of making a living. But it was eventually taken up by Alston Rivers, Ltd. and published in 1906, when Margaret was twenty-one years old, and, much to everyone's surprise, not least of all the author's, it became a bestseller.

To avoid possible confusion—her mother wrote under the name Campbell—*The Viper of Milan* was published under the name Marjorie Bowen, the surname being taken from her maternal grandfather, Charles Bowen Ellis (1821-1887), who was a Moravian minister and missionary. Margaret later wrote that the decision had not been hers; she had wanted to write under her own name, and 'this use of two names unfamiliar and even slightly distasteful to me helped to divorce me from my own work.'[10]

By the end of October 1906, only two months after *The Viper of Milan's* publication, demand for the book was so great that a sixth impression had already been published, and lending libraries were forced to increase their orders for it by the day.[11] And as a result of the success of her first book, 'the literary sensation of the autumn season',[12] Margaret received a cheque for sixty pounds—

the money going straight to her mother—and entered into a new contract with the publisher for two more books. Mrs Campbell ceased the little work she had been doing to support herself and her children, and Margaret became the family's only breadwinner. However, her income was not enough to keep four people, and she found herself 'harnessed to a career of hard work,' forced to 'chase every odd five-pound note in order to keep up with expenses.'[13] Loans had to be repaid, her mother's friends had to be 'helped', and her sister wanted singing, dancing and riding lessons; before a year had passed, her earnings had been spent. And nobody was happier for it; in fact, Margaret felt that they were

'Miss Marjorie Bowen',
The Tatler, 12 September 1906.

unhappier than they had been before. Mrs Campbell was bitterly jealous of her daughter's sudden literary success, having failed to achieve any for herself.

Shortly after the publication of *The Viper of Milan*, Margaret's father died; he had been found dead in the street, with his wife's address in his pocket. His wife, though they had been separated for some years, went to pieces and never recovered from her loss. And Margaret, desperate to gain some freedom from her increasingly difficult and volatile mother, returned to Paris. She found that she could write there easily, and she began to make a life for herself, away from the stifling influence of her mother. But Mrs Campbell was not about to let her daughter break away; she followed her to France and insisted she return home.

The Viper of Milan was followed quickly by two more novels, both successful, *The Glen o' Weeping* (retitled *The Master of Stair* for the US market), published in 1907, and *The Sword Decides*, published in 1908. Yet no matter how hard Margaret worked, and no matter how much she tried to please them, her family remained unhappy and ungrateful. With more money coming in, though never enough to meet their expenses, they moved to 55a Maida Vale,[15] near St. John's Wood, the ground floor of which was occupied by the London and Provincial Bank. Life there was 'untidy, humdrum, and unsatisfactory', and the 'atmosphere was one of constant nervous hysterical storms and tension.'[14] Additionally, the house was haunted, so much so that Mrs Campbell arranged for an expert from the Society for Psychical Research to stay there and investigate while the family escaped to a cottage in Cornwall.

It was at this time, while her family were preoccupied with ghostly goings on, that Margaret met Zeffrino Emilio Costanzo, a Sicilian who had lived in London for several years. Her family did not like him, and she liked rather than loved him, but he offered a means of escape; he was going back to Italy and might be there for some years, and he wanted her to go with him. And despite her mother's opposition to the match—she opposed the removal of the family breadwinner—Margaret and Zeffrino were married in the October of 1912. Zeffrino was given a position with a company that was building a railway in the Carrara district of Lucca, and the following year the couple set out for Italy, taking a furnished house in Lucca Reggio, a two-hour train ride from Florence.

At the beginning of their married life in Tuscany, the couple lived on Zeffrino's income; his wife's earnings continued to support the Campbell family in London. However, when the railway in Lucca was completed in 1919, Zeffrino lost his position and fell ill as a result, and the couple were forced to live on Margaret's income from writing. In an effort to reduce their outgoings, they moved to Florence and took an apartment in a large farmhouse near Santa Margherita. Their rooms were uncomfortable, and Zeffrino, who by then had acquired a constant cough, became increasingly violent-tempered; Margaret felt that all her hopes for a new, different life, away from the petty arguments and miseries of life with her mother, had been crushed. Then, on 4 August 1914, they received the news that England had declared war on Germany.

Margaret and her husband made attempts to get back to England, but their efforts came to nought. The banks restricted withdrawals almost immediately; it was possible to get enough money for basic living expenses but nothing more. Food prices increased, there were riots in Florence, and receiving accurate news from, or sending news to, England was next to impossible. In October, now heavily pregnant, Margaret journeyed with her husband to Sicily to his family home; she grew fond of his father and sister, but she detested the island itself, the way of life there and the disputes that everyone around her seemed to be embroiled in. As she had remained the sole breadwinner of her family in London, she had continued to be productive throughout her marriage—she had produced two or three novels per year since the publication of *The Viper of Milan*—but now she had difficulty acquiring paper to write on or the time in which to use it.

Following the birth of her baby daughter, Giuseppina, on 6 November 1914,[16] Margaret became determined to return to England,

and she and her husband finally began the long and arduous journey three months later. They arrived in London one wintry day in February 1915, and Margaret found her mother and sister much as she had left them. There was no place for Margaret's new family with her old one, so she and her husband moved into a farmhouse above the Kentish marshes, taking old Nana with them, and Zeffrino took up poultry farming. But during the cold winter months his health deteriorated.

On 19 May 1915, after a very brief illness, Giuseppina, then only six months old, died,[17] and Zeffrino was so affected by the loss of his daughter that his health deteriorated further still. In the hope that milder weather conditions would be beneficial, Margaret arranged for them to move to South Devon. She had continued to write— she was, after all, the only breadwinner for two families now—and was receiving an income which, though not quite as good as it had been before the war, was enough to sustain them. But it was shortly after their arrival in Torquay that she received two pieces of news: she was pregnant for the second time, and her husband would live no more than six months if he did not return to the warmer climate of his homeland. So, in October, Zeffrino sailed for home while Margaret remained in Torquay, awaiting the birth of her second child, Michael, who was born the following January.[18]

One month after Michael's birth, Margaret received bad news from her husband; he was more seriously ill than she had thought, had fallen out with his family in Sicily and moved to Tuscany, and he wanted her to go to him with their baby son. It was, of course, impossible to take a newborn baby on such a journey, so she left Michael in England and travelled to Italy alone. She nursed her husband, with very little help from another soul, until his death. Zeffrino died from tuberculosis on 5 November 1916 at the Villa

Ceciale, in the sea town of Forte dei Marmi, in Lucca.[19] Margaret returned to England at the beginning of 1917, to the infant son who, after so long a separation, did not recognise her as his mother.

The little family left Torquay and moved to Hampstead Heath, and, in the October of the same year, Margaret entered into her second loveless marriage.[20] Arthur Leonard Long was aware from the beginning that his wife did not love him—'her story and her feelings had been fully explained'[21]—but the marriage appears to have been fairly successful; it was a 'singular and pleasing union, to end only with their deaths.'[22] Her second marriage produced two sons—Athelstan was born on 2 Jan 1919,[23] and Hilary was born on 24 June of the following year[24]—both of whom, along with their half-brother, Michael, she schooled at home until they were eight years old.[25] As with her first marriage, her second was supported by her writing income, and, as she had done since the publication of her first novel, she remained incredibly productive. In December 1921, Margaret's mother died, and from then on she was responsible for the support of only her own household.

On 3 December 1952, Margaret suffered a fall on the parquet floor of her bedroom. She took to her bed and, according to her youngest son, her condition appeared to improve for a while, but on 22 December she collapsed, and she died the following day in St. Charles Hospital, Kensington. She had suffered a haemorrhage due to having fractured her skull during the fall.[26] She was sixty-seven years old. At her death, she left behind more than a hundred and fifty novels and two hundred short stories.

Margaret employed several pseudonyms during her career; in addition to her most well-known pen name, Marjorie Bowen, she wrote as Margaret Campbell, Joseph Shearing, Robert Paye, John Winch and George R. Preedy. These appear to have been adopted

Margaret at her Kent home with her three sons: Michael (left), Athelstan (right) and Hilary (centre). *The Graphic*, 3 November 1923.

to set certain works apart from those appearing under the Bowen name. According to an article entitled 'Alias' in the May 1932 edition of *Good Housekeeping*, the Preedy pseudonym was invented to allow her to write about subjects that might disturb readers of Marjorie Bowen. In several other articles, she explained 'I became bored with the success of very early years. I felt I was living on another's reputation, so changed was I from the girl who had written "I will maintain!"'.[27] Whatever the reason, it appears that there was some effort made to conceal the true identity of the author for several years. *The Tatler* reported in 1952 that, a few years earlier, 'these pseudonyms were among the most jealously guarded secrets of the publishing world.'[28]

As Joseph Shearing, Margaret wrote historical novels with a true crime element; these were described as 'evil, sinister, ghostly, strange, baleful, terrible, relentless... and malevolent.'[29] The first Shearing novel, *Forget-me-Not*, was published in 1932, and from the moment of its appearance there was 'a definite and devoted cult of readers of this writer.'[30] However, a decade after *Forget-me-Not* appeared, Shearing's true identity was still a matter for conjecture; he was 'one of the impenetrable mysteries of the day'.[31] It wasn't until 1942, when *Twentieth Century Authors: A Biographical Dictionary of Modern Literature* was going to press, that Margaret confessed to the fact that she and Shearing were one and the same person.

Margaret wrote two novels as Robert Paye: *The Devil's Jig*, which appeared in 1930, and *Julia Roseingrave*, publshed in 1932. *Idlers' Gate* was published under the name John Winch in 1932. The first title published under the name George R. Preedy was *General Crack*, which came out in 1928, was a bestseller and set the literary world speculating; who was this talented young man? The next Preedy title was *The Rocklitz*, which was published in 1932; yet still, the author's true identity remained a mystery. That is, until *The Rocklitz* was made into a film, and some reporters spotted Margaret in conference with the producer. The jig was up, and she admitted to being both Preedy and Paye.[32]

An article published in *The Sydney Morning Herald* at the time of this revelation gives us an insight into the author's working methods at this stage in her life. Using an ediphone,[33] which she found 'an inspiring helper', she narrated her story aloud, 'as though she were reading it from a written page'; once the story was completed, she transcribed it to paper, 'developing and colouring characters and scenes' as she went along.[34] She also took inspiration from listening to music; it was while listening to Beethoven's *Leonore* that the story of *Captain Banner*, a Preedy three-act drama, first began to take shape in her mind.

The Devil Snar'd, an eerie tale of supernatural influence, was first published as a small paperback 'ninepenny novel' by Ernest Benn Ltd. in June 1932. It was published again the following year, this time as a hardback by Cassell, in *Dr. Chaos and The Devil Snar'd*. In it, Grace Fielding and her husband, Philip, have taken a house—Medlar's Farm—at a remote spot in Northumberland to get away from London and repair their broken marriage. Philip is in love with Angela Campion, an actress much younger than himself, but Grace will not give her husband a divorce, and Angela will not have him without the prospect of marriage. Philip, a well-known author, intends to use the dark history of Medlar's Farm—a tale of adultery, jealousy and murder—to write his next book, but Grace, already unwell due to the strain caused by her husband's affair, begins to see parallels between her own story and that of the murdered woman, Susanna Vavasour, who she believes is guiding her actions. As Philip works on his manuscript, his behaviour becomes more and more suspicious, and as Grace's mental state deteriorates, a tale of adultery and marital discord soon becomes one of jealousy, obsession and murderous revenge. It is a 'low-toned, menacing horror' and, according to the *Daily Herald*, a 'ghost story fit to stand beside *The Turn of the Screw*.'[35] The author 'devoted much pains to the creation of an atmosphere suggestive of a constantly menacing fate, and has achieved a considerable success.'[36]

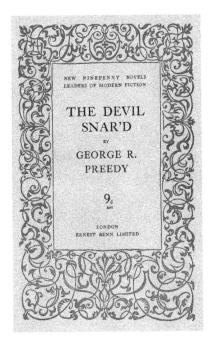

NEW NINEPENNY NOVELS
LEADERS OF MODERN FICTION

THE DEVIL
SNAR'D

BY

GEORGE R.
PREEDY

9.
net

LONDON
ERNEST BENN LIMITED

Margaret achieved a great amount of success during her lifetime; her books sold extremely well for years and several of them were adapted into films and plays: her 1928 Preedy novel *General Crack* was adapted as the film *General Crack* (1930), starring John Barrymore, and her 1939 Shearing novel *Blanche Fury* was adapted as the film *Blanche Fury* (1948), starring Stewart Granger. And yet, most of her titles are currently out of print. *The Devil Snar'd*, like so many of her other works, has never been republished following its 1933 appearance alongside *Dr. Chaos*. It is my hope that the publication of this edition will revive interest in the work of Margaret Campbell in all her splendid masks.

Notes

1 *1939 England and Wales Register.* for the date.
   With regard to her name: The *England & Wales, Civil Registration Birth Index, 1837-1915* and the *National Probate Calendar* record her name as 'Margaret Gabrielle', while the *England & Wales, Civil Registration Death Index, 1916-2007* and the *1901 England Census* have her down as 'Gabrielle Margaret'. Numerous death notices referred to her as 'Margaret Gabrielle Long'. I have chosen to refer to her by the name she chose in her own autobiography: Margaret.

2 Margaret Campbell, *The Debate Continues: Being the Autobiography of Marjorie Bowen* (Heinemann, 1939), p. 9.

3 Ibid. p. 7.

4 Ibid. p. 11.

5 Ibid. p. 65.

6 Ibid.

7 Ibid. p. 79.

8 Ibid. p. 84.

9 Ibid.

10 Ibid. p. 91.

11 *Daily News* (London), 19 October 1906, p. 4.

12 *Daily Mirror*, 8 September 1906, p. 5.

13 Op. cit., Campbell, p. 95.

14. Ibid. p. 102

15 *Census of England and Wales. 1911*, Paddington North.

16 *UK and Ireland, Find a Grave Index, 1300s-Current.*

17 Ibid. Giuseppina Costanzo was buried in the churchyard of St Mary the Virgin, Stone-cum-Ebony, Ashford, Kent, England.

18 *England & Wales, Civil Registration Birth Index, 1916-2007.*

19 *England & Wales, National Probate Calendar (Index of Wills and Administrations), 1858-1995.*

20 *England & Wales, Civil Registration Marriage Index, 1916-2005.*

21 Op. cit., Campbell, p. 290.

22 Ibid.

23 *UK, World War II Allied Prisoners of War, 1939-1945. WO 345.*

24 England and Wales, Death Index, 1989-2021

25 Gertrude Mack, 'Marjorie Bowen: A Triple Personality' in *The Sydney Morning Herald*, 27 August 1932, p. 9.

26 *Belfast Telegraph*, 29 December 1952, p. 1.

27 For example: *Torbay Express and South Devon Echo*, 27 December 1952, p. 5.

28 The Tatler, 13 August 1952, p. 13.

29 Stanley Kunitz and Howard Haycraft, *Twentieth Century Authors: A Biographical Dictionary of Modern Literature*, H. W. Wilson Company, 1942, p. 1272.

30 Ibid.

31 Ibid., p. 1271.

32 Op. cit., Mack, p. 9.

33 A recording device for oral dictation where sound was recorded on a wax cylinder. The machine marketed by the Edison Records Company was trademarked as the 'Ediphone'.

34 Op. cit., Mack. p. 9.

35 2 June 1932, p. 13.

36 *Northern Whig*, 10 May 1933, p. 11.

"It must be admitted that these cases are very perplexing. We might, indeed, get rid of them by denying them, but the instances are too numerous, and the phenomenon has been too well known in all ages to be set aside so easily."

Mrs. Catherine Crowe, "The Night Side of Nature."

"We must next remember, that this earthly body we inhabit is more or less a mask, by means of which we conceal from each other those thoughts which, if constantly exposed, would unfit us for living in community; but when we die, this mask falls away and the truth shows nakedly."

Ibid.

THE DEVIL SNAR'D

Mrs. Fielding knew from the first that this was a frightful journey to an unknown destination, though her ticket was from London to a Northumberland station. She looked from the train window at the strange landscape over which the twilight was darkening down and saw a solitary swan on a black pool; for the first time a sight of this beautiful bird seemed to her a presage of some fearful event.

"For which of us?" she said aloud; and she looked at her husband, the only other occupant of the carriage. He appeared to be asleep, but his stern, unrelaxed attitude showed that he was merely feigning in order to be rid of her company; it was a long while since he had felt any pleasure or even any ease in being alone with her. Thick shadows that seemed to leap in from the gloomy countryside invaded the carriage, but neither of them roused to switch on the light.

Mrs. Fielding tried to struggle with her abominable thoughts; this effort left her as exhausted as if she had undertaken some difficult physical strain; her head was lolling with fatigue against the stiff cushions as she thought fiercely to herself: "I am only tired and depressed. Of course we are going to be happy again—now, or never——"

Her senses ached into a half-delirium; a travesty of a childhood game came into her mind; her fingers plucked at the travelling-rug over her knees as if she pulled the petals of a monstrous daisy from the yellow heart: "Now or never—now or never——"

The words beat into the rhythm of the wheels and throb of the engine that was bearing her North—towards Medlar's Farm.

*   *   *

After they drove from the small, lonely station, Grace Fielding had been preparing herself to give an enthusiastic welcome to the house that her husband seemed, in advance, infatuated with; it was desperately necessary that she should please him. But when they arrived she was too tired to do more than smile assent at the arrangements the housekeeper had made.

Besides, her husband never asked her opinion.

"A beautiful view, ma'am," said the housekeeper, holding the curtain apart for a moment to show the Northumberland hills and dales receding into the twilight, and she named several famous places quite unknown to Mrs. Fielding, that could be seen from this room if the day were fair.

"A queer old house," smiled the traveller faintly. She was exhausted by the long emotional strain she had undergone, by the re-action of a sudden and dubious victory.

"Very old, ma'am, parts of it. Norsemen built some of it, they say. But the west wing isn't above two hundred years old. Mrs. Holmes wasn't sure, ma'am, if you'd want the whole house, or some shut up, being only two of you? I did my best, but the orders was rather vague."

"Yes, I haven't been very well; I had to leave everything to my husband—you know———"

"Ah yes, the gentlemen don't think of such things—do they? But now you're here, perhaps you'd say, ma'am."

Mrs. Fielding tried to clear her head, to recall practical affairs; it had mattered nothing to her what was or where was the house that her husband had taken; all that concerned her was that they should go away, at once, anywhere, together. All she knew was that he had told her he had found a place in Northumberland, belonging to a Manchester cotton merchant, which they might have for three months in good order with housekeeper and servants—fairly cheap, too, though money was not one of their problems.

She felt the mild disapproval of the efficient woman who was waiting for her reply, but she could not force herself to do or say anything practical to-night.

"My husband writes," she said, knowing this well-worn formula would still cover much. "I expect that he would like to choose the rooms himself."

"Perhaps you'll look over them, ma'am, when you've had a cup of tea? There'll be time before dinner. I mean, I don't know where to make up the beds, or anything."

"Yes, we'll decide then. I really am rather tired."

"Tea is quite ready, ma'am."

Mrs. Fielding had her tea alone in the largest drawing-room with the bow window, which was expensively furnished; she remembered something about "careful tenants, no children" in the advertisement that her husband had shown her. She tried to combat a sensation of loneliness, of strangeness, of dislike for another woman's possessions and atmosphere; to concentrate on the fact that Philip had surrendered to her passionate claims and come here with her, alone, far away from Angela Campion and her maddening influence. A triumph, and when she had been almost sure of defeat. But she could feel only lassitude; what an odd thing fatigue was, damping down the strongest passions, leaving only one desire, that for rest, rest, rest.

The journey had been comfortable, not too long. Of course it had not been the journey—it was that devastating struggle with her husband which had begun when she had discovered that he was in love with Angela.

She wondered now how she had had the tenacity to sustain

such a conflict, in which she had, after all, played a poor part, humiliating, mean, ungenerous, unwise.

The housekeeper brought a message that "Mr. Fielding was seeing the luggage in" and that she "was not to wait."

"Yes, we have brought a good many things, books and pictures. Perhaps you will take my husband a cup of tea—wherever he is?"

The housekeeper lit the lamp and left the room. Mrs. Fielding had noted with some dismay that there was neither electricity nor gas in the house; she liked town life, she liked comfort, the very name Northumberland smacked, to her, of barbarism. She had had enough of rough ways when they had been poor; it seemed a shame now that they had the money——

She broke off her reflections, angry with herself—discontent was not for her, nor fatigue—and what weakness to think of victory as triumph—the hardest part lay before her—she had to consolidate her gains, to please, to propitiate, to be infinitely tactful. Philip might, even now, suddenly return to Angela—how could she, Grace, judge of the security of her tenure? His surrender had not been so warm or so eager as to make her feel safe for ever. He had seemed more to recognise the justice of her claims than to acknowledge the strength of his own affection or of her charm for him.

It was June, but she was glad of the wood fire. She had not realised how much later the seasons were in the North—as they drove from the station (what a long way off the railway was) she had noticed that many of the thick hawthorn trees had not yet fully broken into bloom.

"I think, Grace, they want us to look over the house; are you too tired?"

Her husband was speaking to her across the shadows; he seemed very far away as he stood in the doorway. It would take her, being used to a flat, some time to feel easy in these vast rooms.

"No; I'm quite ready." It was difficult to be entirely gracious without cringing, or seeming to cringe, for she was in the position of one receiving favours. She perceived that everything was going to be difficult until she was quite sure that he was not regretting Angela, not sacrificing himself to his duty, to his compassion.

"Do you like the place, Grace?"

"I think I do—very much. But I have really seen nothing of it but this room."

"It's very curious. Unique, I should think. The last house in England they tell me."

"The last house?—oh, Scotland, of course—but I didn't know that we were so near the border."

"We aren't—the point is, that it's all heath, hills, open country——"

She followed him into the corridor, the housekeeper was in front with a lamp. He still wore his heavy tweed overcoat and looked, she thought, very tall and massive; he seemed quietly excited; at reunion with her in this solitude, or because of the crazy old house? She knew that he was capricious, absorbed in violent imaginations, full of an energy, a curiosity, that nothing could exhaust or assuage —a brilliant mind, a wilful, impatient character, great gifts. She only half understood him, though she had thought of little else but Philip Fielding since she had married him fifteen years ago.

"I must learn to like this house if it fascinates him," she thought. "I must get the history, the plan."

She tried to speak with animated intelligence—"What was the house, really—Medlar's Farm? But not in the least like a farm."

Mrs. Mace, the housekeeper, gave low-voiced information— no, not a farm, the dower-house of a big estate that had long since been sold out in parcels. The great mansion had been pulled down a hundred years ago—Vavasour, the name of the family, you could see their tombs in the old abbey, and that was only a ruin now— no, she could not tell how the name came, the land had been farmed for a generation, but she didn't know that the man's name was Medlar; she came from Newcastle and had only been with the Holmes for two years—they were abroad, at least, Mrs. Holmes and the children were, Mr. Holmes was looking out for another house for them to return to in the autumn.

"Why?" asked Philip Fielding.

"Well, sir, the children aren't strong. It is rather a gloomy place for them, and there's very little company, and a great difficulty with the maids, and Mr. Holmes thought he'd like to be nearer his place of business—it was only week-ends he could manage here, sir."

"I see. So the old place will be for sale?"

"I suppose so, sir."

They passed through a door that led to the head of a stairway. Mrs. Fielding immediately saw herself in a mirror that hung to her right hand, a mirror so dimmed that it might have been smoked. After all, she was glad of the lamplight, the shadows; she looked tired, middle-aged; she was glad, too, because of her good figure, her fine taste in clothes. Her graceful bearing, her costly, uncommon garments made her, she knew, attractive, even when dishevelled and fatigued—but why concern herself about her appearance? Philip was not looking at her; she tried to concentrate on the house.

They had passed into the Georgian wing; the unlit well of the stairs was hung with ugly, dark eighteenth-century portraits; on the landing where she stood were several mirrors, old Bible boxes, wig stands, uncomfortable chairs, wooden pattens, and warming- pans of tarnished brass.

"Junk," thought Grace Fielding as Mrs. Mace described how all these "antiques" had been found by Mrs. Holmes in the attics and barns.

"There is a lot more, ma'am, all manner of old stuff; a few years ago no one seemed to care about these things, and now everyone is after them."

"I suppose the Holmes bought the place furnished?"

"Yes, sir, all the furniture goes back to the Vavasour's day—except the room where Madam had her tea, the Tudor room they call it; Mrs. Holmes had that furnished to her own taste."

"And mine," thought Grace. "It is the only possible room that I've seen yet." She said aloud, "This part doesn't look as if it had been lived in for a long time."

"Well, no, ma'am, ever since I've been here it has been shut up —Mrs. Holmes preferred the older part, the Viking house, the children used to call it—that's why I was anxious to know if you wanted this opened———"

"Oh, we couldn't—use this wing, I mean—look at the state it is in———"

"It is quite clean, ma'am, the girls have so little to do, the house being empty, I keep it all ready———"

Philip Fielding, as if impatient of these feminine debates, went down the stairs into the dark, and the housekeeper hurried after him with the light.

The shadows fluttered down the stairs, pursuing the lamp. There was, for all the boast of Mrs. Mace, a smell of must, of damp. Mrs. Fielding wished that she were at home—no, home had been spoilt for her by the fearful scenes that had lately taken place there, they would move when they returned to London—wished, then, she was anywhere but here. It was no use, to-night she could not even enjoy the thought of her uninterrupted companionship with Philip. She was tired; now she was away from the fire the house felt cold.

She followed her husband and tried to take in something of the rooms that Mrs. Mace showed them; but the house remained a chaos—seemed to her to have no definite plan; it had been so often rebuilt and added to; half the Georgian portion had been burnt down, the remaining rooms were too large for the proportions of the facade she had seen on driving up from the station. She counted dining-room, library, writing closet one side of the passage; two withdrawing rooms connected by folding doors and a lady's boudoir on the other; then kitchens, cellars, cupboards below in a dim subterranean region which she refused to inspect; and, above, four large bedrooms, a closet changed into a cheerless-looking bathroom, and, above again, attics. All the rooms were handsomely furnished with an uncomfortable confusion of objects. To Mrs. Fielding, used to a neat modernity, the whole place was like a museum; she was not insensible to the dignity and beauty of the various pieces of walnut and marquetry, the pictures, tapestries, candelabra, and vases that overcrowded these stately rooms, but she had no interest in the past.

"Do you like this better than the older part, Grace?"

Her husband's voice startled her into a sharp realisation of his presence; he had seemed merged into the shadows of the house; she had seen his figure looming ahead of her, lit by the dim lamplight, and scarcely known the tall man as Philip; she was fatigued to the point of hallucination.

"I saw nothing but—the Tudor room, don't they call it?"

"It is very queer, like a ship—slate floors, heavy timber."

"Ship's timber it is, sir, so they say."

8

"This part is more civilised. You don't like low ceilings, do you? Wouldn't you feel more at home in the big room upstairs—with the chintz?" He looked at her kindly, she was sorry to need kindness.

"It seemed so cold—that big room——"

"I could soon have a fire, ma'am."

"Very well. Of course you are right, Philip."

His consideration for her increased.

"Wouldn't you like to go there—at once—as soon as they can get a fire? It isn't so frightfully cold. Mrs. Mace will send up some dinner."

Mrs. Fielding smiled. No use pretending, she was absurdly tired; the strangeness of the place was depressing, she had slept badly for so long now, and surely she was, for a while, safe. He would give her at least a few days; he would not abandon her cruelly... suddenly....

To distract herself she said, as she mounted the dark, dismal stairs:

"Naturally, the house is haunted?"

"They say so, ma'am, but I've never seen anything. There are old stories. I'm a stranger, as I said, and I don't encourage the girls to gossip. You can soon get a place a bad name."

"Especially a place like this," smiled Philip Fielding.

Grace Fielding was not frightened by ghosts; they belonged, in her opinion, to the dimmest realm of fairytale. She was not troubled by such remote terrors; she was completely absorbed in her own averted tragedy—was she quite sure that it was averted, or only held in abeyance?

*   *   *

She woke suddenly after deep draughts of sleep that she had snatched at greedily, and thought, at once, that it was strange that she should rouse herself in this complete silence, when she had been so utterly fatigued. It was alarming to realise that she was in such a state of nervous unrest that even exhaustion could not long hold her in blessed oblivion.

Another sleepless night; she lay resigned in the strange four-poster bed with the hanging of coarse twill embroidered by the hand of some dead Vavasour with indigo-blue flowers and red foxes. A night-light burnt on a side table and the embers on the wide hearth still glowed; through the half-drawn curtains showed a rift of ice-blue moonlight; the shapes of large pieces of dignified furniture were blurred by shadows. Mrs. Fielding felt her surroundings to be very stately and impressive after the impertinent prettiness of her London rooms; though this chamber was alien, it was soothing.

She tried to fix her thoughts on something agreeable: Philip's kindness last night—that now. He had been almost tender when he had said "good night"; he was asleep in the next room, a door half open between them, surely it rested with her to bring about a complete reconciliation—in this solitude.

But Mrs. Fielding could not, for long, keep her thoughts peaceful. What was that small kindness last night, a mere matter of courtesy perhaps, compared to the bitter brutality that had gone before? His strained voice, demanding his liberty, still echoed in her ears; he had pleaded with her—to set him free for Angela. She had, through all these storms, held firm.

"I can't prevent you leaving me—but I can prevent you marrying Angela. I won't divorce you. I won't give her everything. While I live you shall never marry her."

She was startled to find that she was sitting up in bed, saying, half aloud, these words that she had repeated, so often, with the dreadful tenacity of despair.

"But I was right," she muttered, casting herself back on the pillows. "I was right not to give way."

Angela played at virtue; that was what was intolerable. She wanted to be respectable, to have a good social position, to have the glory of being the wife of a famous man, to go everywhere with Philip, showing off her sham beauty, her odd gowns, her lisping wit; to share his fame, his popularity. On that dreadful day when she had come to see Mrs. Fielding she had as good as admitted this fearful greed.

"I inspire him; I'm really needful to his work; it's only right that it should be acknowledged. He'll go to pieces if you don't take care—it's a strain for him, you now. I wonder you don't see that you are being stupid."

"You're stupid too. Philip has only been famous, making money, for five years; for ten years I helped him, poverty, sickness, tempers, moods—he had all my money, that was useful too. You came along when he was rich, well-known, good-humoured with success. You can be his mistress if you like, but you'll never be his wife."

They had descended as low as that, quarrelling, bickering, over her husband; why must she remember it? Those ugly sentences would not be effaced from her mind, nor those flushed, distorted features, puckered with spite, of the other woman. How was it that Philip, so acute, so sensitive, could not see how trashy Angela really was? That she had nothing but her mediocre beauty, her quick cleverness, her eager self-confidence that seemed like talent. But how useless to speculate on what a man saw in another woman. Angela was young, seductive, shameless, full of vitality, an ardent flatterer; no doubt her lure was simple enough.

Mrs. Fielding flung herself out of bed: "This torturing restlessness! I hope that I am not going to be ill—that would turn it all to ridicule. Philip, of all men, with a sick woman on his hands in this place."

The room was warm; she sat on the edge of the bed, trying to steady herself, and only fell into the last mistake of weakness, that of self-analysis.

Why had she clung so desperately to a man who did not want her? Because she loved him? Ah, no doubt she did, but she was long past knowing what love exactly meant, and there had been times, during the last months, when she had both hated and despised him.

Because she was afraid that, in losing him, she would lose everything that made life pleasant and exciting? She had passed her fortieth year; she had no talents; no one ever seemed to want her for herself, but as her husband's wife she was very welcome everywhere. Was she afraid of giving up her share in the fame she had helped him acquire—of falling into the background, of being merely a divorced woman whom people pitied?

She was flicked by imagined comments: "Poor thing! But one can hardly blame him, he must have felt her a drag, and then Angela Campion is so brilliant—and it isn't as if there were any children—and I believe that he has been very generous with the money——"

Her clamouring thoughts clotted and festered round the word "money." They had been poor so long; she had sold out her little capital to give him the leisure in which to write the things he wanted to write; she had rescued him from hack journalism; she had given up her own work on the stage to help him, to become his servant, his adviser, his clerk, his secretary, to be the butt, the shock-absorber for all his moods, his despairs, his tempers. No children —her barrenness—that had seemed a virtue, a blessing then, now it was a vague reproach, a dim curse. Angela was smiling with an opulent promise of fecundity. No doubt Philip would be flattered

12

by children in an expensive establishment with plenty of servants —but in the old days, in two rooms, in one room, children would have been the last touch of sordid horror—they would have made what was already bitterly difficult, simply impossible.

"Why am I going over this? I was trying to think why I won't let go—it is an obsession. There are other men in the world. I'm not a fool; surely I might find interests for myself—why do I cling?"

Because, perhaps, of sheer loathing for the other woman, that greedy, insolent, shameless thief, who had laughed in her face and just snatched Philip like someone might grab your bag in the street?

Perhaps.

She could not deny that to have foiled, to have humiliated Angela gave her a savage satisfaction; she liked to imagine that final interview in which he had said some equivalent to "good-bye."

But ignoble emotions can give, she thought, very little ease; the jealousy, the struggle was a torment, it hurt, sharply, to hate.

She left the bed, nearly stumbling over the unexpected old-fashioned bed-step, and put on her white wool dressing-gown; a bracelet of many-coloured gold winked on her wrist as she moved near the night-light; it caught her attention, for she was not yet used to costly objects. And her mind turned again to money. How suddenly it had come—a success in America, the play, a novel, lectures, films; there must be fifty thousand pounds behind them, and handsome contracts ahead.

It seemed incredible.

"Behind us? It is all his, really. I suppose, if we did separate, he would be generous. Angela has money. I should take all I could get. I have a right."

A right? Had she? Because she had shared his poor fortunes, toiled for him? She had *liked* doing that; the eager service, the joyous hope of the future; his moods of passionate gratitude, his entrancing companionship, the fact that he always remained her constant lover, had made her happy—how mean to think of exacting payment for that——

She moved to the door of his room and listened; she could not even hear his breathing.

Why had he brought her here? She became suspicious—perhaps it was not, as he had seemed to promise, to affect a complete reconciliation, a renewal of their old relationship, but to persuade her, in this solitude, to let him go; to plead with her, to argue with her, to wait until she had, as he would think, recovered from the fatigue of the scenes in London, to shame her by all the forces of logic and all the strength of passion, into giving way.

She took up the night-light and crept into his room. It was long since even this extent of intimacy had united them; since he had been sleeping in the "spare" bedroom at the flat she had never entered it; and he had been away so much, at his clubs, in the provinces, anywhere, any excuse.

Shading her small light she looked at herself in the mirror that hung inside the door before she looked at him, and her tired eyes were bright with self-defence.

"I am not dowdy, I am not old. I can hold my own with anyone. It's something, even nowadays, to be well-bred, decently educated, and Angela is common."

But Angela had hair like the floss newly unwrapped from the cocoon, and a gentle red mouth, lovely in shape, that required no lipstick, and a complexion that nothing seemed to ever fleck or flaw. The reflection at which Mrs. Fielding gazed so keenly was that of a dark woman, not ill-looking, graceful, with fine eyes and richly growing hair, but a woman who had lost all her lustre, all bloom, who looked, even in a half-light, burnt out.

She moved to the bed, another four-posted with stiff needlework curtains and carved pillars, and stared down at Philip.

The obvious soundness of his sleep vexed her and made her envious. She thought that he, too, should have been tortured with insomnia. Was it not strange that he took the parting from Angela so lightly? And her suspicions returned. There was some trick in this abrupt, this almost careless, surrender.

She did not, to her own surprise, look at him with devouring affection, but with compassion, almost with contempt.

"Poor Philip."

He looked older than he was. He would soon be heavy, even stout; sagging lines showed round eyes and mouth, a fullness under the chin, his handsome hair was a little grey at the sides, a little sparse on top. When he was asleep all his attractiveness, his comeliness, seemed to eclipse.

Her gaze wandered to the unfamiliar pattern of his sleeping suit. She remembered, not so long ago, when she had known every stitch in every garment he possessed, so often did she wash and mend them. She glanced at his clothes, flung down untidily; at the little table on which were his watch, his pocket-book, his keys, a heap of coins. How soundly he slept, or how quiet she was! He did not stir as she picked up the pocket-book and peeped inside. Several of Angela's letters; she knew the thick, impetuous writing, the crisp peach-coloured paper. She might have guessed. She was afraid of the sharp crackle of the notepaper or she would have read these letters. They were addressed to his club.

A small dispatch case stood at the side of the little table; he had, she thought, placed it there carefully, well within reach.

It was locked, but it did not take Grace Fielding long to select the correct key from the cluster on the side table. She found within more letters, several photographs of Angela, a small bottle of colourless fluid, with a label on which was written in a strange hand "Headache Drops," together with some odd papers, pamphlets, and books.

Mrs. Fielding closed the case without interfering with anything. She had never, in any way, spied on him, read his letters, followed him, searched his pockets, yet it was not shame that made her pause now, but fear of his awakening.

"After all, there is nothing to it. He would be sure to keep her letters—her photograph. I'm as uncertain as before—it wouldn't help if I read what she has written. Will she write again—here? There's no telephone. And he can't go out casually to meet her. But I suppose she'd think nothing of coming to Newcastle or— what is the nearest town? What shall I do if business suddenly calls him to London? I must not keep turning all this over or I shall lose all control, go half crazy."

She retreated from the bed, taking the little light with her, shading it with her hand. Seen through the shadows, he looked grand, noble, in his sleep. How could she have despised him just now? Her mood was all tenderness; even his remembrances of her rival seemed merely pitiful, childish.

She passed on tiptoe to her own room, closing the door after her, thinking vaguely, dully, of the white swan she had seen from the train.

Of course I can't let it all go by default. He can't just drop into a quiet friendliness—shut me out, while he dreams of her. I must have an explanation." Like an echo came—"another scene."

The fire was very low in her room, it gave neither heat nor glow; the night-light was dying in her hand; the flood of moonshine that slid between the curtain was a purple-green that startled the town-bred woman; it seemed off that never before had she realised the colour, the strength of moonlight.

"Another scene? But I can't, I won't give way; I must find out why we came here—if he is genuine or only playing." She sat musing on the edge of the bed again, and her veering mood was once more tender.

"Poor fellow, he has been suffering too—those headache drops —he is generally so indifferent to those things, but he remembered to bring them." She smiled wistfully. "In the old, bad days, as he calls them now, he never had headaches."

*   *   *

They met at breakfast, which was set in the Tudor room. Mrs. Fielding had already been over what Mrs. Mace named the "Viking House," the old portion of Medlar's Farm, and hated it— dark, gloomy, every possible inconvenience, slate floors, heavy beams, little crooked stairs, little twisted rooms with small windows, a multitude of low doors, every bit of comfortable furniture looking sadly out of place....

"Philip, that ancient part is out of the question, I simply can't be bothered with it—but we could be quite comfortable here. If you agree, we'll just shut that up and move everyone over here——"

"Did you tell the housekeeper that?"

"Yes, I did. She seemed very disappointed. I can't think why— that part must be very tiresome to run—the kitchen is appalling. No wonder there is a difficulty with servants."

"But you're safe there, Grace. I made sure of that before we came. There are two girls under Mrs. Mace—one is the wife of the chauffeur, Hicks, the other is his sister; they live in a cottage by the fruit garden. Then there is the gardener's wife to fall back on, in the next cottage—all these people are permanently engaged by the Holmes, as good wages, and would put up with anything to keep their places."

It was most unlike Philip to take any interest in domestic affairs, to be so exact over trifles.

"Funny for you to bother, dear. And why should they have to put up with anything? It seems to me that we shall give very little trouble."

Philip Fielding was silent; his wife was vexed by his musing air, his inattentive look, but she was careful not to show any impatience.

He was suddenly, eagerly speaking.

"Grace, there is something I ought to tell you."

She sat rigid—a confession—Angela—the real reason for their coming here....

"I saw Holmes in London when he came up on business——"

"Mr. Holmes! What has he to do with it?"

"It is his house."

"Oh, you're talking of the house!" She was both relieved and disappointed.

"Of course. Holmes was quite frank about it. The place has a nasty reputation. He can't live in it—can't let or sell it—probably they'll pull it down in the autumn—if I don't buy it——"

"Ghosts?"

"Yes. The very ancient part is all right, even the ghosts have died of old age, I suppose. It's this wing. You won't get Mrs. Mace to come here much—she sleeps in the cottage, you now, we are quite alone at night."

That pleased her, real solitude—and an excuse for her to demand that he never left her....

"What attracted you about the idea, Philip? I didn't know that you were interested in ghosts!"

"Not put like that—just ghosts! But—the other side of things, atmosphere—suggestion—always! And I wanted to get away, really away. When I saw the place————"

"I didn't know that you had been here before————"

"Yes, those few days I was in Birmingham—I just ran over. I was going to say that the very sight of it made me realise how disgustingly banal a rut we had got into—the sheer cheapness of one's own little moment, little interests, the chatter, the money grabbing. I want to do good work, Grace."

"Can you do it here?"

"Yes. It is a real get-away isn't it?"

"Oh, that, yes! I feel cut off—from everything."

"We are. Isn't it a relief?"

"Will the ghosts help you write, Philip?"

"I dare say. I've got so many ideas in my head, poems, plays—I do want them unspoilt. I'm really afraid, Grace, of writing for money. It's so insidious—a temptation—to please the American market, the film market, the general public! Agents, publishers, managers, getting anxious—for fear you let them down. I wanted to get away."

"Well, here we are!" How long could he be so impersonal? Was there to be nothing to clarify their relationship, no promise, no pact? She must be patient.

He continued eagerly speaking, without conceit, with rather a touching lack of self-confidence, with a genuine humility, a real desire to avoid the false values that so speedily surround success. But she was weary of this delay in their complete understanding.

"Well, you need not worry about money, Philip. And if you like the place and feel you can work here—there is nothing against it, is there? Only," she rose, making a light question into a direct challenge, "what am I to do all day?"

"You always seem to find plenty of interests, Grace."

"In the old days when there was work for me, yes—and, in town—before we disagreed—yes; but here? With plenty of servants and no society—utter loneliness, isn't it? And I'm not a woman for long walks with dogs or helping in the garden——"

"I thought that you, too, wanted to get away——"

"From London? From Angela?"

"Among other things——"

"Is it that, Philip? Did you really bring me here—to make a clean break?"

"I thought you couldn't stand any more of it. You couldn't, you know."

"I can't stand it here, either, if I'm not sure."

She held on to the back of the oak chair, feeling that her pose was theatrical, her voice harsh, and not able to alter either.

"How sure do you want to be, Grace?"

"I thought I'd made that clear—we simply can't go over it again —as if I could! But just to come here——"

"Isn't it enough?"

"You know that depends on you."

She had always been thankful that he had never tried to fence with her, to use any verbal quips or evasions, those maddening confusions of words that torture like darts of wild fire and come to no conclusions.

He said now, simply: "Angela and I—we shan't see each other again. She is going to Africa, on a long tour." As his wife did not answer, he added anxiously, "That makes it all right, doesn't it?"

"Yes. Oh, I suppose, yes." She crossed to the fireplace, sat down

on the padded fender, trembling; he came and stood over her.
"What is the matter, Grace?"

"I feel such a beast."

"We were all rather beastly."

"Even Angela?"

"Of course, Angela too. It wasn't the sort of thing that could happen without making everyone—beastly."

"I know." Tears lay in her eyes. "That is why you should never have begun it, Philip. We have always been rather lofty, you and I—and then—you did bring us down with a bang, didn't you? You made me show the very worst of myself." She smiled wistfully. "I don't believe I'll ever forgive you for that."

"It's so difficult to forget," he said quietly, as if he agreed with her self-contempt. She was deeply stung. It did not need much for her smouldering wrath to flame, but she kept herself in hand.

"Of course we've discussed things that ought never to be mentioned—and lost self-respect, horribly. It was worse for me—I was so acutely humiliated——"

"Don't——"

"But I want to say that I wasn't really always in love with you, Philip. I quite despised you, often—but I wanted the position, the money. And I—*disliked*—Angela, it was so obvious that she would make any man—a wretched wife."

It seemed to her that she had salved her tattered pride by these foolish words—which she did not even know the truth of; he was looking at her, curiously.

"Well—that's reasonable. And now that Angela has cleared out—you'll be happy here?"

"No, Philip, it isn't reasonable. Nothing is reasonable." Tears of sheer weakness were running down her face. "And I can't be—

happy—anywhere—till things were like they used to be——"

"You'll upset yourself again. Poor child, can't you stop crying?"

"Not easily—it was all such a ghastly shock."

"I've been punished too. I feel a fool, a prig—oh, I don't know —Grace," he took her arm abruptly. "I've got through it—we're here together, help me to get straight again——"

She stared at him, winking back her tears.

"Why do you look at me as if you didn't believe me?" he demanded.

"You gave way so suddenly. Are you sure that Angela didn't just get tired of waiting and sent you off."

"I don't think," he said sullenly, releasing her arm, "that we ought to talk of Angela."

"No? Why not? I suppose she—you—used to discuss me—oh, what am I doing? Our first morning and I am spoiling everything!" Her distress was so piteous that he said at once:

"Never mind, dear, we'll get along all right. You're overtired; you ought to rest for days and days. We'll go motoring a bit, the air is excellent and there are some wonderful places round here."

She should, she knew, have been satisfied with this poor substitute for the passionate lover's reconciliation that she desired; but she had not the strength to resist saying:

"You're kind. But if I was to say—after all—you can have your divorce—I suppose you'd wire Angela not to sail for Africa?"

She did not like the queer breathless tone in which he counter-questioned: "But you won't?"

"No, I won't."

*   *   *

Mrs. Fielding found that there was even less for her to do at Medlar's Farm than she supposed—the house "ran" itself. Mrs. Mace organised everything, and there were really no neighbours. The nearest house was shut up; it belonged to wealthy people who were hardly ever there. The nearest village was merely a group of cottages, a church, a school. Medlar's Farm was far off the high road, and the village was well away from even the motor-coach route. Mrs. Mace mentioned that the only "good" doctor lived twelve miles away—not much for a car, of course, but, with no telephone, no wonder that Mrs. Holmes, burdened by young children, found Medlar's Farm too lonely.

Grace Fielding would have preferred to have lived in the cottages by the large walled fruit gardens; they were cosy and cheerful, with just the pleasant air she associated with the country. She liked Hicks and his wife, the pleasant young sister and the baby, the cat, dog, and poultry, everything there was sane and normal. In the big house it was not—the maladjustment between herself and Philip seemed to affect everything.

The entry of Mrs. Mace to end and already delayed breakfast had interrupted their conversation at a dangerous point:

"But you won't?"

"No, I won't."

He knew, at least, that she would not give way. He had made no further attempt at an elucidation of their position, nor had she; her fatigue was like a barrier between them. He said continually, kindly, that she must rest, and left her, under that excuse, much to herself until she wished that she had never confessed to fatigue.

Of course this could not go on for long, these lonely nights, these merely friendly days, but he continued to hold her at bay, and she was exhausted, content to drift awhile on the placid tide of this imitation happiness. She had, after all, some satisfactions—Angela did not write, for Mrs. Fielding saw all the post that came to Medlar's Farm. Perhaps Angela had already sailed for Africa. Why had Grace Fielding not felt a throb of triumphant joy at that news? because she had not really believed it. This renunciation had seemed too sudden. She could not question the strength of his passion—and yet he had been able to relinquish the object of it so suddenly.

She watched him suspiciously, knowing all the while what a foolish thing it was to do, but could not detect any uneasiness on his part. He appeared absorbed in his new book, and deeply interested in fitting up the old library as a work-room. In the brief evenings he would talk, brilliantly, enthusiastically, of his plans—poems, plays, novels, and she would listen intelligently; on the surface it was like the old days.

He recurred to the subject of the reputation of the house.

"Do you mind, Grace? I thought you wouldn't——"

"No, I don't; I wish I did. It would be rather an excitement. I'm sure there are ghosts, and sure that I shan't see them. The past is quite dead to me."

"Doesn't this house, the things in it, mean anything to you?"

"I feel that it is gloomy, rather sad, quite out-of-date——"

"You don't have any sense at all of the people who used to live here?"

"No—do you?"

"Not exactly—but I want to——"

"Why, Philip?"

"It's so tremendously interesting. There is a lot in that sort of thing, I'm sure, despite all the rubbish encrusted round it. I would like to—get in touch——"

His words were, to his wife, incongruous to his appearance, his character; he seemed, in everything, worldly, there was nothing of the effeminate dreamer about him, he had been a good soldier, was a good sportsman; perhaps it was foolish of her to connect poetic effeminacy with spiritual matters.

"Why did you want particularly to come here, Philip?"

"Well, for the solitude—and then, the story—one of the stories of the place—is exactly the same as one I've been wanting to write —when Holmes told me that, I felt I must come. Of course it is only an experiment—but it would be extraordinary if we could get through—really—take the stuff down as it were—direct from one of the real people."

"Which story is it, Philip? You've told me so many lately."

"Not this one. I can't yet. I don't know it myself. I have to wait till it comes, bit by bit——"

"But the facts? What Mr. Holmes told you?"

"Oh, just a rather ordinary murder."

"I see."

"Sure you don't mind?"

"No. I suppose there have been murders in most old houses —and worse horrors than murders. I'm not a sensitive person, as I keep reminding you. But I do think it rather odd that you——" She broke off abruptly; was it so odd? Perhaps this passionate throwing of himself into a new interest was not so odd, perhaps it was his way of trying to forget Angela. "What are these ghosts supposed to be?" she added, though she was not really concerned at all in that aspect of the affair.

"I won't bore you with them. They are rather a tangle too—so many and, I believe, quite unusual. Mediums have been here and exorcists, all no use. Holmes admitted that he only advertised on a desperate chance—he wanted to keep the servants on till the autumn; they suit him, and so on. He put in 'no children,' you remember?"

"What did he see himself?"

"Nothing much. Rather a farrago. But it's got a nasty name. No doubt," he added with relish, "the worst haunted house in the North of England."

"The servants don't say anything."

"Honour bound, eh? And a bit scared too. I shouldn't question them."

"I don't." She thought stupidly: "But I shall have to question you, things can't go on like this."

*   *   *

A few timid walks, a few swift drives in the car, gave Mrs. Fielding an impression of a country that seemed to her far more alien than any foreign place that she had seen; hills, lakes, open plain, lonely roads, a few far-scattered farms, a few small villages, grey, sombre, without flowers or orchards, not in the least like the villages of the south. Stone walls instead of hedges; a wide, distant, tumbling horizon; a cold, thin air, and, the farther one turned north, an increasing bleakness of landscape, of weather. Grace Fielding had always had an aversion from chilly desolation, and this country seemed to her desolate indeed. Even the masses of June flowers could not, she thought, soften the grim outlines of the hills, the barren effect of the moors; the sweet flowering grasses, the lovely blossoms were so small, the landscape so large. She did not like to see the hawks hovering high in the cold-looking remote upper air, and every turn in her walks or drives would bring suddenly to her hostile gaze a vista of some unutterable melancholy, distant, other worldly, lit by some wild gleam or steady radiance that reminded her of the awful landscape of the Apocalypse.

Yet she preferred abroad to the house. Not that she had any sense of atmosphere or contacts with the dead, or with sinister spirts who had never been alive; not that she concerned herself with any of the stories of the place (being too self-absorbed to care), but the dark, rambling stairways, the unfamiliar rooms and old furniture, combined to depress her, and she was bored, too, by lack of any occupation. It was all very well to say "rest"; but idleness was not rest. While she lounged in an easy chair, her hands slack, her head sunk in cushions, she was thinking, furiously, her mind racing round the problem of herself, Angela, and Philip.

A problem that, she was sure, had not been solved by this exile in Medlar's Farm.

Philip was kind, but no more. He put up his work as a defence —that and her presumed fatigue. He behaved as if he had never loved Angela, but he also behaved as if he had never loved Grace.

He was not altogether reserved; she was allowed to help him by dealing with such of his official correspondence as his secretary forwarded from London; he continued to discuss his work, his plans—how desperately she wished that she did not feel that all this was part of a barricade against her, that she did not detect in all he did and said a certain hollowness, a bright falsity—"Or am I imagining that? Have I been so tormented that I can't become sane again?"

She gloomed and brooded, her passion turned inward by his withdrawal from that final reconciliation, that complete renewal of their love that alone could have assuaged her long bitter tumult of soul. In those moments (every day becoming rarer) in which she was able to see herself with a detached judgement, she feared that the well-spring of her life had been corrupted by the struggle with Angela, and that poison would flow for ever through all her being, even through her dreams, which were always seething with doubt, dread, and suspicion.

*   *   *

Mrs. Fielding came into her husband's study holding a glossy society weekly. He was surrounded by books, by maps, prints, drawings, and a confusion of small articles, pipes, a pair of mittens, a wig stand, some skates, an odd stirrup—all old, clumsy, tarnished.

He had, she noted, rearranged the books in the heavy oak cases; many of these were tumbled out on the floor—such large, heavy books on such ponderous, forgotten subjects. The summer landscape, a corner of the garden, the dipping, tremulous line of remote hills, that showed through the tall, uncurtained window, seemed to belong to another world from that of which the room was part.

"Seen any ghosts, Philip?"

"I wonder." He was good-humoured. "I'm getting it, anyhow, a suggestion here, a line there—all these things," he pointed to the objects on the large table, "belonged to *them*."

"To *them*?"

"I see." She glanced at the shrunk mittens, the ugly spur. "A man and a woman."

"Well, yes——"

"Which was the victim?"

"I'm not going to tell you." He smiled. "When I've got the story clear, I want you to guess the end. Besides, I'm not quite sure myself."

"Neither am I, Philip. Sure of what?"

"Sure of the murder——"

28

"It must be a queer sort of story if there is any doubt———"

"It is—there are two stories, you see." He seemed really enthralled, delighted by his secret thoughts; common sense told her that he was not acting, yet she completely distrusted him. "I shall get them both, I feel certain—the stories, I mean, and the people as well—all here, telling me everything. If I could only get materialisation."

"You haven't—ever?"

He did not seem to notice the listlessness of her tone.

"Well, yesterday, nearly. I was reading of *them* lost on the mountain, in the mist, and I did feel my feet wet, dripping from the long grass, and then, suddenly, there was a portion of a brocade sleeve near my chair. I could see the pattern, the threads of the material, the outline of the figure was being built up—then, nothing!"

"I mustn't forget that you are a very accomplished writer of fiction, Philip. What is the theme of this complication?"

"Jealousy." He spoke with a maddening impersonality, as if he did not know the name of the passion gnawing at her, day and night. "Stupid," thought Grace Fielding, "or cruel?"

"I see." She placed on the table the magazine that she held. "I see, too, that Angela isn't going to Africa."

"Oh, I didn't know." He glanced down at the open page which showed Angela, cunningly photographed against a gauzy background, delicious in a wide hat and roses. The caption stated that "this beautiful and accomplished actress" was shortly to appear in a West End production.

"It may not be true—and, Grace, do you much care if it is?"

He looked at her steadily; there was not much feeling in his question.

"I shouldn't care—other things being equal," she muttered. "But———"

"Tell me what is wrong——"

"This house, this country——"

"You aren't getting scared?"

"Oh no! Ghosts, all that sort of thing doesn't exist for me—haven't I told you—often enough? But it's dull, gloomy, alien—and you so absorbed. Couldn't we go away. Italy? France?"

"We could. But not just yet. I want to get this work in hand. I'm sorry, but *I* like the place."

"How soon could we go away?"

He considered a second. "A month? Say, the middle of July? If there is anywhere one could go—quietly—in July——"

Instead of rejoicing at his speedy surrender to her whim (for so it must seem to him, she knew) her suspicions increased. Why did he give in, as it if was not worth while to dispute with her?

"A month is too long," she said sullenly.

"Well, sooner, then—give me a week or so. I can come back here in the autumn, if you hate the place——"

"Come back?"

"Yes, I've made up my mind to buy Medlar's Farm—it's a ridiculously low price. And I couldn't endure to think that it should be pulled down—why, that would be enough to make the ghosts haunt one indeed."

"I don't think, Philip, that it would matter if it was pulled down. It's strange that you like it. I can't understand how it can—soothe you. Don't you ever get headaches here? It's so aimless."

"You know that I've never had a headache in my life."

She thought of the small bottle with the label that she had seen in his dispatch case, and she smiled.

"I can't stand much more of Medlar's, Philip."

"Well, you go on somewhere, and I'll follow——"

She tried to thrust aside all the reserves, the shames, the doubts, that tried to strangle her love, to speak directly to the man whom he had been.

"Oh, Philip—let us go away—together. This place isn't right. Leave your work for a little—let us try——"

"A second honeymoon?"

These were the first words in bad taste that she had ever heard him say; he spoke tenderly, yet the short sentence made her see herself as withered, middle-aged, greedy of affection, even—lustful.

She left him, the portrait of Angela by his hand, and he turned to his books as if the interruption had been of little moment.

* * *

At dinner that evening Philip Fielding spoke pleasantly to the housekeeper.

"Mrs. Fielding doesn't like Medlar's as much as I do, Mrs. Mace. One of these fine days she is going off—leaving us."

"I'm sorry to hear that, sir. I hope that Madam hasn't seen anything, I always said—that Georgian wing——"

No, no—nothing of that kind. She is simply bored, and I mean to send her off somewhere a bit brighter and follow on—I can't leave just yet. I suppose that you could look after me for a while, Mrs. Mace?"

"I'd try my best, sir."

"You do everything now," said Mrs. Fielding. "I dare say that is why I find it dull. But I don't suppose that I am likely to run away quite as soon as my husband seems to think——"

"Don't you listen to her, Mrs. Mace—I'm expecting her to fly off any day now——"

When the housekeeper had left the room Grace Fielding asked:

"Why did you tell her all that? Nothing is settled about my going away."

"But you might want to, suddenly—and there is no need to let her think that we have quarrelled. Besides, I really wanted to know if she'd put up with me, alone."

"It's unlike you, Philip, to be subtle and far-seeing——"

"Is it? I'm only just the average fool always."

*   *   *

When Mrs. Fielding again visited the chauffeur's brick cottage she asked:

"What *is* the story of Medlar's Farm? I mean, the one that makes people refuse to live here? I hear that it must be pulled down if my husband doesn't buy it?"

"Well, ma'am," the young woman evaded, "it is a lonely, inconvenient sort of place——"

She was awkwardly embarrassed; plainly this was a forbidden topic.

"But what does it matter now, Mrs. Hicks? So long ago! And I'm sure that you're not afraid of ghosts any more than I am?"

The other gave her a searching look.

"I don't know, I'm sure, ma'am. I always like to be indoors when it's dark——"

"Well, what is the story? Some murder?"

"Yes. A horrid murder—a man and his wife—he murdered her——"

"That's not so uncommon——"

"But they were gentry. I don't rightly know the tale, and I did promise I'd not speak of it. Mrs. Holmes said that one keeps these things alive by speaking of them——"

"I mustn't ask you, then. Poor woman! You might tell me her name, I suppose? Is she buried in that ruinous old abbey?"

"Susanna Vavasour her name was—and she's buried in Crompton Old Church—the one that'll be submerged when they finish with the lake for the waterworks. And that fits in with the old stories, too, for she said she'd never sleep till the Resurrection, and they are moving all the bodies before they drown the church."

*   *   *

Mrs. Fielding's habit of stealthy spying on her husband had increased. She found little to reward her, but one day, creeping into his study, she found an interrupted letter on his desk—

Dear Angela,

Don't write again—not until I've done what I set my hand to——

So Angela wrote to him, though not to the house. Of course he was frequently out in the car and could easily pick up her letters at any village post office.

*   *   *

Mrs. Fielding's patience broke; under some trivial excuse she made a scene, as fierce, as pitiful as any she had made when he was at the height of his passion for Angela. At first he was soothing, compassionate, then stern and angry, finally goaded into retorts, but at last, in a hasty agony, he had resworn his old vows: he did love her and Angela was nothing: everything should be as it had once been: yes, they would leave Medlar's Farm: yes, they would go to Italy, in a few days, if she wished.

What more could even her greedy jealousy wish?

When she dragged up to her room, he did not follow her but sent the housekeeper to look after her. Mrs. Fielding, really ill from emotion, lay broken in the Tudor bed, pleading a sudden nervous attack, thinking to herself:

"It is all false; he means nothing of what he says—he is too kind, he gives way all along the line, he is far more considerate than he used to be—why all this trouble? When one embrace, one kiss, would be enough——"

She took a sleeping draught as a desperate escape from her misery, and woke in the middle of the night. She was cold, bewildered, and felt, as she moved, sick.

More like a sensation than a thought there ran through her consciousness: "Something is wrong—with me—with the house; everything is worse than it was in London. Is it possible that these dead people are really impressing me, influencing me, filling me with—despair? For why should I despair? The situation belongs to me again, if only I could handle it. But I can't. Why do I disbelieve everything he says? Take no comfort from his promises, his kindness? He even asked Angela not to write again—until he had done what he had set out to do. A reconciliation with me, he meant—a complete reconciliation."

She sat up in bed; the night was warm, there was no fire, no moonlight, the night lamp flickered heavily; the door between their rooms was closed.

Insomnia again; the sleeping draught had had little effect. How foolish to isolate oneself here—so far from a doctor or even a chemist.

Her nausea passed, leaving her charged with hectic energy. She sprang from bed, half dressed, took the lamp and went downstairs, indifferent to the darkness that her little flame only feebly scattered, with no aversion from the loneliness of the shut-in stairs with the bleak portraits.

She entered the study and began to turn over her husband's papers, searching for some letter to or from Angela, some clue to the labyrinth of his soul. There was nothing, neither letter, note, nor diary. She wondered if she dare steal into his room and open the dispatch case again. And stood irresolute, staring at the piles of books, the pages of paper, covered with a fine, hurried handwriting.

She had never taken a keen personal interest in his work; her joy, her pride, her labour, had all been for the man, not for what he had accomplished. She would have rather, indeed, that he had expressed himself in action, for she had a faint touch of the primitive feminine contempt for the poet, the artist.

But then, as there was nothing else for her jealous scrutiny to feed on, she began to turn over the pages of notes for his new work— she did not know it if was to be poem, or play, or story.

The first sheet she took up was headed—*Susanna Vavasour*, and was covered with rough jottings.

"The crime was so exquisitely planned as to be impossible of detection. No one will ever be quite sure."

"Her ravaging jealousy might have driven a better man to a worse deed."

"He found the other woman a harassing difficulty—he had to rely so much on her patience and discretion; and every day he longed for her more and more. Yet the thought of his utter freedom—so soon to be achieved—kept him calm, even cheerful."

"A simple, tasteless, odourless, colourless liquid—cyanide of potassium. He had arranged, cunningly, about the servants. Nothing could be more lonely than their situation."

"Could she not have forgotten her danger? No, jealousy caused a kind of aberration in her usual acute brain———"

Mrs. Fielding put down the sheet of foolscap. A huge spider was running over the rubbed leather books shown in the circle of the night-light; she watched it, a speeding blot, hasten into the shadows that filled the entire room, leaving only herself, a few sheets of paper, a fountain-pen, and the murderer's iron spur visible in the wavering yellow glow.

*   *   *

Mrs. Fielding returned slowly to her room, holding on to the high, polished ramp with one hand, while the lamp shook in the other.

"If one believed in guardian angels—what instinct sent me down there?"

She was very cold, but neither frightened nor appalled. It was all so logical—no doubt it had been planned from the moment that Angela had given her that contemptuous warning—"If you don't take care, he will go to pieces."

An aberration indeed, but now it had gone; the congestion in her brain was relieved, she neither loved nor desired Philip, she was neither bewildered nor suspicious. She knew. It was all so logical, everything fitted in so exactly. She sat on the edge of the bed again, the light on the side table.

His sudden surrender, his attempts to soothe her, the choice of this desolate spot that no one wanted to live in, that he was going to buy—and shut up. "I might rot in one of those awful cellars for a hundred years and no one come near." All the domestic arrangements, the solitude at night, the difficulty of getting a doctor, the fact that no one locally knew her, no one would miss her, his preparation of Mrs. Mace for his wife's sudden disappearance, the headache drops, concealed in his case, the unfinished letter to Angela—"what I have set my hand to———"

What a fool she, stupid, jealous, loving Grace Fielding had been, to dream for a second that she could separate those two. She would not give way, so they had planned to destroy her. While her wretched body that he had once caressed lay corrupting in this cursed spot, Angela, sleekly triumphant, would become Philip's wife.

Like the last gleam of light in a stormy sky before the sun is finally obscured came the thought: "Of course this is all ghastly nonsense. I'm brain sick—Philip isn't a murderer! No, nor is Angela. This would never have occurred to me in London, the cheerful flat, the friends—the fame, the money—those were the real things—this is only the awful house and thinking of the story of Susanna Vavasour." But this gleam, which she clutched at as if it were the last spark of sanity in a world of madness, was soon spent; she remained, not only emotionally, but intellectually, convinced that Philip had brought her here to murder her; everything fitted into this belief.

Was he not violent, impulsive, abnormal, like all men with a touch of genius? Did not his work deal, however beautifully, with crimes, cruelties, and the darkest of border lands? Had she not herself often heard him excuse a murderer and declare that every human being was a potential criminal?

She had pressed him too far, and he had decided to be rid of her. Marriage was Angela's price, and he had resolved with all the fury of his passionate maturity to have Angela. It was all very simple. He had, no doubt, been searching for some lonely place when he had seen the advertisement of Medlar's Farm, and the coincidence of the old murder had fascinated him—also the utter security offered by a house in which no one would ever live—which he could buy cheaply and leave for ever deserted without exciting comment.

Ah, it was not all play-acting, his poring over the story of Susanna Vavasour. No doubt he was trying to cloak himself in the personality of the dead murderer, to learn from him how to be rid of a jealous wife.

A tasteless, odourless, white liquid—cyanide of potassium?— what was that?

Mrs. Fielding, very cool and deliberate in her actions, went to her medicine cupboard and took out from a corner a small empty bottle, which she carefully washed. She then shivered into her husband's room, unlocked and searched the dispatch case which he had again left close to his bed. The bottle labelled "Headache Drops" was still there; she opened this, and with great nicety poured the contents into her clean bottle, and filled the original bottle with water from the glass on the bed table.

After she had done this, she looked long at her unconscious husband, screening her night-light with a hand that was quite steady.

He was sleeping rather uneasily, turning from side to side, his face twitching. She noted on the side table a pile of papers and old books relating to the Vavasour case and the history of Medlar's Farm.

How clever he was, how cool. If it had not been for that odd intuition, like a whispered warning in her ear, that had sent her down into the library—he would have completely succeeded in his cunning plan.

But she, too, was clever and cool, and could be cunning. She stared at him without a spark of affection, even with a wonder at herself for all the pain she had undergone on his behalf. She viewed his dark, heavy features with distaste; an old tag jangled in her ears —"love to hatred turned"; what was it? "A woman scorned"... her memory halted.

She returned to her room, gripping the bottle with the liquid taken from her husband's case, and recalled another line of the hackneyed quotation: "Hell hath no fury——"

*　　　　*　　　　*

Mrs. Fielding's quiet, casual insistence had induced the housekeeper to speak of the ghosts of Medlar's Farm. She did so reluctantly, but not without a certain relish in the topic.

"You see, ma'am, it's the *influence*, that's what is so bad. That's why Mrs. Holmes took the children away—the medium they had down here said it was dreadful, pure evil, and that if anyone was a sensitive, as they call it, or ill, or in trouble, it would be very dangerous for them to come here——"

"You mean that the ghost would get hold of such a person, enter into him, as it were, to do a crime?"

"That was the idea, ma'am—nasty, I call it."

"No doubt, Mrs. Mace, it is very nasty. Have you ever heard of such a case among the people who have lived here?"

"Well, ma'am—there's talk, you know, Mostly suicide, as if the poor things were trying to escape—but, there, I mustn't chatter. While you're living here, you won't want to hear these old tales. And I dare say that it is all nonsense."

"But you wouldn't care to sleep here?"

Mrs. Mace smiled submissively: "I must say that I shouldn't, ma'am, not for *payment*. Though I must say I've never seen or heard anything."

"Neither have I. But all the same——"

* * *

Mrs. Fielding took a fair motor run to a distant town where she had seen "*analytical chemist*" on the bow window of an old-fashioned shop, and stood, formal, smiling, amid the delicate soaps, pleasant bottles of perfumes and lotions, the cases of pretty cosmetics, combs, and sponges.

The agreeable young man behind the decked counter leant forward, all civil attention as Mrs. Fielding approached with her question.

"Can you tell me, please, what cyanide of potassium is? Is it a poison?"

"Yes, indeed! A terrible poison." The young man's candid eyes stared from behind his thick glasses. "Prussic acid is another name for it——"

"Oh yes, I've heard of that. What is it like, please?"

"A tasteless, odourless liquid—or powder—a very little would kill anyone, instantly. It is the quickest poison."

"Thank you so much. I have a friend who said she had got some in Paris—she rather teased me about it——"

"Paris? Perhaps. You couldn't get it over here, not easily——"

"I must get it away from her. How could you use it?"

"It depends what form it is in," replied the young man doubtfully, wondering if he was doing right in giving any information. "I'm not an expert—you'd find it in some book on toxology, you know."

"If she was to pour a few drops into tea or coffee—or—" Mrs.

Fielding's glance fell on the shining array of perfume atomisers—
"spray it down the throat from one of those?"

"Yes; it could be used in a syringe, of course——"

"I dare say it is all a joke—I just wanted to know. I'll look it up—
thank you so much——"

Mrs. Fielding had left the shop before the young man could pass
round the counter and reach the door. She had seemed to him sane
and honest, but her questions had slightly disturbed him. However,
she was a stranger, a tourist no doubt, and it was not likely that
he would ever see her again, and he thought, as he watched Mrs.
Fielding's graceful figure disappear up the street, that if he had been
indiscreet, no one would ever know it, if he himself was quiet about
the dark, expensively dressed woman and her unusual questions.

* * *

Mrs. Fielding met her car at the public parking place. She did
not wish Hicks to know that she had been to the chemist's shop;
an old castle was her excuse for two visits to the distant town. She
congratulated herself on the adroit quickness that she was acquiring.

On the long ride back she hugged and turned over her knowledge,
as if it gave her an aching pleasure, like pressing a throbbing wound.

How did one get poison? She did not in the least know. She
had heard of arsenic in rat-bait, sheep-dip, weed-killer, but this one,
more deadly stuff, in a neat bottle? What did it matter? Philip knew
everyone, went everywhere; no doubt he would find no difficulty....
She remembered an enthusiastic acquaintance with a man who
specialised in poison mysteries.

* * *

Philip Fielding, after days of easy good-humour, fell into a peevish gloom; the weather was wild, dark, and rainy, his work had "stuck." He was not sure, after all, that he liked the atmosphere of the place—it *was* sinister and—rotten.

"Confound these Vavasours and their ghastly crimes—it's about got over me. Musty and stinking. I wish I had never begun. And such a puzzle too. All the crucial parts of the records seem to have been purposely defaced or destroyed."

"Going to give it up, Philip?"

"I think so. You're right—this place is no use. Let's get away—Italy?" He placed his hand on hers and looked at her with what seemed the most candid affection; she sat immobile—"He's jibbed it[1]—or—remorse?—or—another plan?"

"What on earth are you staring at, Grace?"

"Oh—a great spider, passing along the wall just behind your head—I never saw such a large one———"

"I thought you'd seen one of those tiresome ghosts—at least!"

She laughed with that hearty loudness so uncommon in women of her type. Philip, continuing to press her hand, seemed pleased.

"You've got your spirits back, Grace, anyway, however much you dislike the place———"

That evening their reconciliation seemed more complete than it had been since Angela had enticed him away. But she had no pleasure in this; she judged him clumsy, tiresome, and viewed with malice all he did.

*   *   *

---

[1] Jib: To be unwilling to do something.

And in the morning, to her bitter, secret triumph, his mood was changed. He would not immediately leave Medlar's Farm; he had got over his disgust of the Vavasours and their crimes; the story was, after all, piecing itself together in his head.... To Mrs. Fielding this was the unmasking of a villain. She was savagely pleased by his exposure (as it was to her). After this, no doubt of his purpose entered her mind, which became focused in this central fact—that he had brought her here to murder her, calling in, with tricky cowardice, the aid of a long-dead murderer. Nothing fantastic in that, grotesque as it might seem. Even scientific researches admitted, as a commonplace, that awful and violent deeds left behind them a hideous force which haunted the scene of their unnatural actions, and which could seize on to a receptive person exposed to its influence.

Mrs. Fielding had no doubt whatever that her husband shut himself up in the library day after day, not to write his story, but to invoke the dead murderer, to summon him to his aid to commit a similar crime. She remembered how intensely interested in mediums Philip had been a few years ago, and that he had himself undergone some training in occultism.

Of course he had learnt a few tricks.

She felt no concern in the original story, only in its effect on Philip. She did not wish to fumble round the details of the ancient murder, to pore over old books and dingy pictures; she asked no more questions about the history of Medlar's Farm, either from the servants of from her husband, who must by now, be an expert on the subject. But she had the curiosity to visit Crompton Old Church, where Susanna Vavasour lay buried in a grave that would soon be disturbed.

*   *   *

The large lake, Crompton Old Water, was in the hands of the engineers; the head of it had been already devastated and disfigured by a colony of temporary iron dwellings for the workpeople. Mrs. Fielding passed a school, a club, a dance hall, rows of neat cottages, women and children going about their work and play. The church, she was told, was at the other end of the lake, a walk of two miles. That and the vicarage were already shut up, there was nothing much to see... but Mrs. Fielding set out along the lake side where path soon became little more than a bridle track.

She found it astonishing to observe how soon the large activities of the engineers were left behind; after half a mile there was no sign that this, the wildest and most remote of the lakes, had ever been disturbed. To her left cascades of wild flowers and a few delicate trees bordered the water; to her right, beyond a belt of brambles and tall weeds, rose a sloping hill scattered with sheep. The loneliness was complete; there was not a boat nor a bird on the dark surface of the lake, and the hills beyond shut it into isolation.

Mrs. Fielding passed neither human being nor animal—a derelict farm gate in a sudden broken wall of stones was the only sign of human handiwork.

The day was fair, cloudy, with a faint milky vapour high in the heavens and a sunshine that seemed to fall through veils of mist from very far away. Wild thyme, mint, and heather gave a fragrant sharpness to the air; the towns-woman noted, even through her abstraction, the tall perfection of the unimpeded weeds and unblemished blooms of white, yellow, and red. She did not know the names of any of the flowers (save the buttercups), and lovely as the strange blooms were, they added to the alien atmosphere of the grave landscape.

When she reached the abrupt turn of the lake, there was the church, hidden in yews, and, opposite, the vicarage with shuttered windows in a neglected garden. Beyond, the path straggled into the wild hill-side and disappeared. It was impossible to proceed any farther; the other side of the lake was inaccessible, for a thick growth of trees rose from the verge of the water.

Though she had taken the car as near as she dare to the lake head (for she was secretive about her wish to visit the church), Mrs. Fielding was fatigued by her unwonted exercise. She sat down on the bank beneath the vicarage gate and ate some chocolate that she had brought with her. The loneliness penetrated deep into her being; the shut-up church, the empty house—were far more emblematic of solitude than the lonely land and water. The people who had lived here, been buried here, had left behind them a heritage of utter isolation.

Here was not only the loneliness of nature's utter indifference to humanity, but the loneliness of humanity's own futility and frustration.

Mrs. Fielding's soul became stripped of all that was of little moment in her existence. She cared for nothing save for what was associated with her hatred of the two people who had robbed her and then planned to destroy her. She was no longer concerned, even with her own escape, which she could easily achieve by merely leaving her husband, but solely with the consideration as to how she could most injure them—Angela and Philip——

She could not think, even in her concentrated malice, of any better way than that she had already employed—of refusing to release Philip, of refusing to give to Angela the triumph of being his wife.

She would hardly be able to continue living with a man who was watching for a chance to murder her (yet she felt herself capable of thwarting him even in this), but she could, somewhere, *live*, and thus defeat them.

She rose, haggard, graceful in the expensive clothes for which

Philip had paid, and passed into the churchyard. The gate in the brick wall was swinging on rusty hinges. When she had passed this she found herself in a tangle of shadow from the yew trees that crowded round the small, decayed church of native stone, and seemed to gather all the graves into their darkness as by an incantation; for in the little space where the sun shone no one was buried, but the even meadowsweet grew waist high.

The church door, sunk in the low porch, was locked. Mrs. Fielding, in sullen vexation, shook the bolts; then turned away with a scowl on her face.

But perhaps Susanna Vavasour was not buried in the church, but somewhere in the blue-black shade of the yew trees.

So, stooping under the flat boughs, peering at crazy headstones, Mrs. Fielding searched the lonely churchyard. There were crosses, mouldering from damp, wooden boards rotted from the sunk supports, long mounds that sent the low lusty weedy that grew thereon higher than their fellows, and presently there was, to the north of the burial ground, an altar tomb, protected by an iron railing that, rusting into decay, had fallen this way and that.

Mrs. Fielding stood and stared at this tomb that stood almost out of the shade of the yews and the barrenness of the ground they grew upon. She could read a few half-defaced letters on the flat table-like stone that was cracked across in two places and bound by the hairy cords of a red-leaved ivy. Susanna Vavasour. Then some Latin that Mrs. Fielding could not understand, some hollows in the stone that still held last night's dew, then a few English words, broken and in an unfamiliar spelling. Mrs. Fielding made them out to read thus:

"For what I did I can answer..."

There seemed no sense in this sentence, but Mrs. Fielding was in no mood to cavil at that. She stood long, half in the misty sunshine, half flicked by the outflung boughs of the yew tree, thinking of Susanna Vavasour. And of the other woman in her story. Had he married her when his wife was—dead? Was he hanged for his crime? She wished now that she knew the details of the old tale.

Though all was so fair and still, her humour corrupted the sweetness of the placid day. She felt the stench of rotting bones that must long since have become one with the mould, and sensed that somewhere near her feet crawled obscene insects, the horrid devourers of dead flesh.

She clung to the railings, and the rust came away in flakes on her gloves, the corroded spikes touched her cold face. She stared at the letters on the dark tombstone, which held, she believed, the secret of Susanna Vavasour.

A white butterfly, greenish yellow at the wing bases, fluttered on to the damp stone and then instantly away. Mrs. Fielding gazed after it, and trembled to think of its destination.

The remote peace of the churchyard was to her heavy with menace; never had she been in a more awful place.

She thrust her hand through the crazy railing and beat her feeble fist on the rough stone.

"What happened? Why didn't you escape? Stupid—to allow him to kill you—and go to her."

She was not surprised at the sound of her own voice; for lately she had got into the habit of muttering to herself, and her words seemed to be at once caught up and involved into the silent threat of the stillness.

She tried to evoke an image of Susanna Vavasour from out the churchyard hush. Closing her eyes she forced her imagination and visualised at once a woman in a tight-fitting bodice of a green that seemed of the very darkness of the yew trees; her face was colourless, neat featured, and a small quantity of pale hair was drawn away from a high, smooth brow. "Of course," thought Grace Fielding, "that is a portrait I saw without noticing it closely—a print on Philip's desk." She opened her eyes and the vision remained; a picture, like a transparent palimpsest,[2] over the still flat boughs of the funeral trees, over the still air.

The woman now appeared to be seated on the tombstone and looking fixedly at Mrs. Fielding, with the almost painful intensity of one who wishes to convey an important message and may not speak.

She was leaning forward, and Mrs. Fielding marked the tarnished silver buttons of braid that fastened the lustreless taffeta across her narrow breast, and that her pale skin had a faintly wrinkled, perished quality.

"It is certainly the picture I saw—if one wishes one can really evoke a phantom—I wonder if it is Susanna Vavasour."

Her eyes were feeling the strain of this long stare at the creature of her own creation, she supposed, for the vision began to waver into ripples of light, like the emanations of intense heat, but, before it had entirely disappeared, Mrs. Fielding observed a large spider crossing the crumpled flesh of the bosom: "Why should that come into my mind now? The same insect that I saw crossing Philip's papers—the night that I found out——"

She moved away from the railings of the tomb; she felt suddenly listless and exhausted; the loneliness and the stillness of the place hung on her like a weight.

---

[2] A manuscript in which writing has been erased and covered by new writing.

She thought of the water soon to be poured by the engineers into the lake, the water that would rise, rise, until it was over the empty church, over the vicarage—what would they find when they opened the tomb of Susanna Vavasour? She would like to see that, a heap of dust, a few yellow fibrous bones. She put her hand on her own arm and thought of her own skeleton rotting in the cellars of Medlar's Farm, while far away Philip lay in the clasp of Angela.

She wandered over the open space beyond the graves and broke down the wild flowers as she went, a trail of destruction behind her.

Nothing more to be done here—nothing to be discovered or gained. Her sullen glance travelled over the church. She was close to a sunken doorway; in the keystone of the arch above it was a curious, clumsy carving that caught her attention. A grotesque fiend with medieval horns and tail was pursuing a thin creature in grave-clothes who turned at bay, and, with an expression of the utmost horror, cast a net over the enemy who writhed in astonished helplessness. Mrs. Fielding thought that the victim who suddenly became the aggressor had a look of Susanna Vavasour in the pinched features.

"Susanna Vavasour? But I've never seen her—yet that image of her was very strong. I suppose that is what Philip does—evokes people like that——"

She turned away, loathing the place, yet hating to leave it; she felt that she had been defeated in the attempt to surprise some secret.

"Now I must go home." Her whole being ached at the word. Home, Medlar's Farm, the alien rooms, the dark stairs, the shut cellars, the shut-up attics, and Philip, watching her, waiting for his opportunity.

As she turned away from the closed house from which the chimney smoke would never rise again, from the church where no more prayers would ever be said, she looked backwards continuously, and her fancy set Susanna Vavasour in her tight, green-black bodice, leaning over the gate of the churchyard, beckoning earnestly to her as if she wished to whisper to her some important secret.

*   *   *

When Mrs. Fielding, tired and moody, turned into the gate of Medlar's Farm, she saw, in the avenue of ancient pollarded limes, a slim, smart, glossy blue car; her muscles became taut—Angela! While she, Grace, had been day-dreaming in the old churchyard that would so soon be submerged beneath the lake, and therefore of no concern to anyone, Angela and Philip had been together.

Mrs. Fielding went directly to the library, and, a little breathless from haste, opened the door.

There was Angela, seated by the table on which was Philip's confusion of books, and there was Philip, standing in the window-place.

Angela had been crying; her hair was bright above her green leather motor coat, her hands, outstretched over the piles of paper, twisted the silk cap that she had snatched off. Almost suffocated by hatred, Mrs. Fielding leant inside the door.

"I thought you'd be back soon," said Philip, without moving. "Angela was in the neighbourhood and thought she'd look us up."

"Good morning," smiled Mrs. Fielding.

Angela gave a glance over her raised shoulder.

"Oh, don't pretend—you know I came to see if Philip could bear it."

"Do you think that he can?"

Angela stood up, and shook back her short hair with a movement that was none the less sincere because she had several times employed it on the stage. She was obviously ready with a flaming retort, but

Philip came forward with authority.

"Look here, we can't wrangle over this. Angela was up in the lakes, and it was quite natural that she should think of coming over here——"

"Quite natural," said Mrs. Fielding.

"And she's going away, at once."

"Oh, you won't stay to luncheon, Angela?"

"Don't be a fool. As if I could take anything from you."

"Except my husband——"

"I gave you an opening there, didn't I?" replied Angela recklessly. "Well, haven't you thought better of it? This must be ghastly for you, too—this awful place——"

"Don't," put in Philip sharply. "I told you that it would be no good."

"I want to hear Grace herself—for the last time. Oh, you can't be so crazy! You'll give us—the divorce——"

Mrs. Fielding continued to lean inside the door. She thought: "I suppose this is my last chance, a kind of ultimatum. If I refuse, I pronounce my own death sentence."

She looked from one to the other, and it did not seem at all incredible to her that she looked at two people who had planned to murder her.... Of course, this visit had been to urge on Philip's flagging courage.... Perhaps Angela expected to find her ill, dying.

"It's nonsense for you to ask me," she said in a loud, harsh voice.

Then Angela spoke the words that had just been running through Mrs. Fielding's brain.

"It is your last chance."

"Of what?"

"Of behaving decently."

Mrs. Fielding shook her head. These evasions and double meanings rather confused her. She looked without pity at Angela's soft prettiness, flushed by a swift drive, by bitter tears—"I suppose she was crying because he hadn't got rid of me yet."

Aloud she said:

"I can't prevent you and Philip from going away together."

Her husband answered:

"You know that Angela won't have that, Grace. Isn't it a case for a little kindness? Angela, you'd better go."

"I've had no kindness," muttered Mrs. Fielding. She watched Angela pick up her motoring gloves and linger slowly putting them on.

"She's asked me," thought Mrs. Fielding, "to be decent, to be kind—if I was either, I should leave them alone together. But I won't."

She followed them to the waiting car. She wondered if Angela was the same kind of woman as the rival of Susanna Vavasour. She saw her look at Philip, and his evasion of her glance.

"There is no need for speech, they understand each other perfectly."

"You'll be all right?" asked Philip, as Angela grasped the wheel. "It's a long drive——"

"Yes, thanks—all right."

And she was gone, with no more than that. Husband and wife watched the blue car glide through the open gates of Medlar's Farm.

When it had disappeared Mrs. Fielding said:

"I suppose that you hate me for sending her away?"

"You didn't send her away. She was just leaving when you came in——" In a tone that forbade her to pursue the subject he continued swiftly: "Where have you been all the morning? I thought you couldn't do these long walks?"

She re-entered the house; she was quite broken with weariness.

"I had a fancy to see Crompton Old Church—the one they are going to submerge. A curious carving there—a fiend chasing a soul who has turned round and netted him——"

"Haven't you seen that drawing of it in the library? It is quite famous—the local name is—'The Devil Snar'd.' "

*   *   *

They sat slackly either side of the deep wood fire that Mrs. Mace had carefully piled up: it was raining again and the June evenings were cold. It seemed, too, that even in midsummer these rooms would be damp and chill. The lamp cast a circle of light over the figure of the man, sunk in a deep chair with his book; over that of the woman, sunk deep in a chair with her idleness. Beyond all was shadow which obscured the pretty modern trifles with which Mrs. Holmes had tried to soften the gauntness of the Tudor room, as the ancient dining-room was vapidly named.

Philip Fielding did not like the room, nor indeed, this part of the house. He had been impatient to return to the library, but soon, and with quite a good grace, had acceded to his wife's request for his company. She lay stretched almost at full length, her hands clasped behind her head, her long body relaxed. She could see little of her husband, for he held up the massive book like a shield before his face.

"Isn't that great tome heavy, Philip; doesn't it make your hands ache?"

"I hadn't noticed it——"

"No? Well, I wish that you would put it down and talk to me——"

The book was not lowered.

"What do you want to talk about, Grace?"

"We have enough subjects—haven't we?"

As he did not reply, she continued:

"Angela. Why was she up here? I thought she had had a new part in London——"

"I believe she is taking a rest first."

"A rest!" laughed Mrs. Fielding. "I should not have thought that she found it very restful to come up here to see you. I never saw her so upset."

The book, at that, was put down, and her husband's stern face looked at her out of the shadows.

"Look here, Grace, we simply can't discuss this. Angela has gone. I didn't know that she was coming———"

"How can I tell that you are not lying?"

"I suppose you may infer so from the fact that I never lied to you before———"

"I wonder. You are so cool, so indifferent, Philip, and yet you ought to be in torture. I can't understand how you can give her up like that———"

"Can't you? Why?"

"People don't. And I never thought that you had such strength of character."

"I have nothing to say, Grace, and you will only make yourself ill if you keep on brooding over these things."

Completely changing her tone she cried, sitting up violently:

"I can't imagine *what* you can see in her. Look at her to-day— so ordinary, so cheap, just like any young woman tearing over the country in a vulgar-looking car. She walks badly too; that's always been against her on the stage———"

Her voice trailed away, extinguished by his silence. He had taken up the book again; she could no longer see his face.

She clasped her hands round her knees, steadying herself by the interlocking attitude:

"Are you reading about the Vavasours, Phil?"

He responded at once.

"Yes, there is a tract on the case, bound up here with some other pamphlets——"

"The case? Was there a trial? Was he hanged?"

"No. It seems never to have gone beyond gossip. There was an inquest, but no verdict. It all seems to have gone by default."

"I suppose that encourages you," smiled Mrs. Fielding.

He looked round the side of the book.

"Encourages me? What do you mean?"

"How near we are to it," she thought; "he almost sees that I know."

"I mean your story, of course, Phil."

"Well, I don't see that it is very encouraging to find all researches blocked—there's been a lot destroyed, purposely, of course. It is difficult, nowadays, to realise the power a family like the Vavasours had—they really could do almost what they liked."

"Convenient." Mrs. Fielding continued to fix her husband with an unwinking gaze from the dark eyes that had lately become so hollow and so shadowed by bistre stains.[3]

"I had a queer experience in that old churchyard to-day—I found *her* tomb, and I tried to shut my eyes and force myself to see what she was like——"

"Did you get anything?" His voice sounded eager; he put the book aside and sat up. Her twitching smile broadened; there was a ghastly amusement in thus playing with him when she knew his secret.

"Yes, but it was just a replica of some print I've seen on your desk. Quite strong though. I seemed to still see her, even after I'd opened my eyes. She was seated on the edge of her own tomb, and trying, I thought, to tell me something."

---

[3] A transparent brown pigment made from the soot of burned wood.

"They always do—but it is so difficult. That is how it happens to me. I actually saw *him* the other evening. You know I told you, the patch of brocade—well that came again—then I built up the whole man—of course there are a hundred explanations."

"Do they matter?" Mrs. Fielding rose swiftly and stood before the fire which made a steady red light behind her thin figure. "What did he tell you, Phil? How he did it?"

"As if one ever got anything as concrete as that! Besides—I don't believe that he did do it." Philip Fielding seemed troubled. "I like him—if he was a murderer, I feel sure that he was justified."

"Justified!" echoed Mrs. Fielding. "So you think that murder can be justified?"

"I've always said so."

"That's bold, Philip." She shuddered, despite the heat flowing about her. The big man was looking at her with the blankness of utter malice, or so she interpreted his stare; she felt then very near her own death. "Perhaps to-night, perhaps any night, he will find that the poison has been changed, and take other means." For the first time since she had discovered his purpose she was afraid and melted by compassion for herself.

"Don't you feel well, Grace? I don't think we ought to talk about these things——"

"It was the fire—foolish to stand so near, the heat on my back——" She lay limply down on the end of the long chair. "Tell me some more—I'm not frightened—of *them*."

He did not appear to notice her emphasis. He sat forward, his elbows on his knees. The wavering shadows, the light from the burning wood, were kind to him and returned to him what physical magnificence she had once so adored, and which now, in the common day, was something blurred and marred. His hair fell finely over his square brow; the flaring lines of the nostrils, the curve of the full lips, the set of the chin, had the pristine purity of line. And in the sweep of his heavy shoulders, the modelling of his sensitive hands, was strength and power. Her heart cried out for her one-time lover that Angela had transformed into a monster. To cover her almost uncontrollable emotion she said:

"Read me what you have done of your story, Philip; it is a long time since you have read me anything of yours."

He acceded at once, and pulled a few sheets of foolscap from the thick leaves of the *Miscellanea*, perhaps he also was eager to escape from the present moment.

*   *   *

"They first met at a ball given at a castle near Hexam. Castle, I say, but the older portion was in ruins and a Palladian mansion had lately been raised there by a nobleman, rich from the plumbago and coal mines of Newcastle.[4] Vavasour was poor and a nobody, younger son of a younger son, seventh son of a seventh son, the old women said. He had been abroad ."

*   *   *

A traveller who had often been forced to beg his way. He had worked, too, and gained much experience. I do not know what whim had prompted this return to his ancient home, which then he had no prospects whatever of inheriting. He was staying at this house which we now know as Medlar's Farm—then it

---

[4] Plumbago: 'black lead' graphite.

was called Vavasour Hall. Susanna was wealthy—an heiress in the old sense of the word—that is, she quartered her father's arms on a lozenge, and would bring honours as well as riches to her future husband. She had never left the north, and was ignorant of much, yet well versed in inherited traditions and womanliness. She had all the externals of feminine grace, and possessed all those small dainty virtues which can be openly extolled. She was, then, as I suppose, twenty-two or three years of age, and people wondered why she had not married before.

"As she entered the ballroom, the walls of which were painted with a design of blue lattice through which hung trails of convolvulus,[5] she immediately saw him. She whispered to her father, on whose arm she leant: 'I will marry that man and no other.'

"She had been told since she was a small child that she might make a choice of a lord and master, but so far no man had pleased her more than very briefly. He, Philip Vavasour, had that external splendour which is rare enough and never fails of powerful effect. Though often decried and denied by the envious and the jealous, yet physical beauty is one of the most powerful things in the world, and Philip Vavasour had it, and with it that air of negligence which refutes all possible charges of coxcombry.[6] He wore that blue coat in which he has been most frequently seen since his death. It was heavily frogged with a fine, plaited bullion braid;[7] there was no collar, and folds of fine muslin were

---

[5] Flowering plants in the bindweed family.

[6] Conceited arrogance or foppishness.

[7] Frog: a decorative loop-fastening on a coat.

swathed round his neck. The pocket holes were very low; he hung a slender sword which he had himself bought in Toledo.

"He was presented at once to Susanna Oldmixon and glanced at her with indifference. She was not unlovely; she had the frail, cold, and precise look, I think, of delicately blown glass or finely moulded china, but to him she was not beautiful nor desirable. He was kind to her because she was friendly and he had been long away from home.

"When they had danced together they stood a while in the window-place which was hung with straw-coloured curtains to keep out the winter air and set with a painted table for cards. He kept his hand long in hers, for she had said that she could read the lines on his palm and must thus trace his destiny.

"With this pleasant excuse they stood together, and she said afterwards, and repeated with a strange persistency, that she could see behind him a rich background, very different from this familiar room. She could sense about him the sea, a very different ocean from that which beat gloomily on the shores of Northumberland or surged in the grey waves of the Solway. This sea was vivid and pure beneath an untainted sky, it lapped against flowery shores, the vision of which filled her with an unbearable nostalgia. While she murmured some hocus-pocus about what she foresaw of his life from the reading in his palm she was imagining herself wandering with him on those untrodden islands where fronds of ferns and palms, green as the green of her grandmother's emeralds which she wore on Sundays to the grey church, hung motionless against a purple sea. She saw about him caskets of jewels and panniers of fruit, and tall white buildings green shuttered against the midday sun, and colonnades of clear marble where rainbow-coloured doves trailed their wings along a pavement where hard orange grains were scattered.

"She saw him moving, at once triumphant and indifferent, among all these bright and beautiful things, and she saw herself as his perpetual companion.

"After a while she dropped his hand, giving up her pretence of fortune-telling, and sat down by the card table and crossed her fingers on her stiff silk lap.

" 'It's true,' she said, 'that I have some gift of second sight, yet I have read very little in your palm, but I feel about you many strange and lovely objects.'

" ' I have travelled a good deal,' he said, without surprise. 'I have taken care to see what was worth seeing in every country to which I have been.'

" 'Do you hate this place?' she asked earnestly. 'The north, I mean. I have always felt alien here.'

"He smiled, shaking his head, with a movement rather like that of a noble mastiff who flicks the water from his face."

*   *   *

Her husband was startled when Mrs. Fielding spoke, breaking his story into splinters like a hard blow cracks ice.

"I don't believe any of it," she interrupted. "It is all a fiction. You don't get that, Philip, out of your old book."

"It doesn't interest you?" he asked drily.

"Oh, it interests me, but a great deal of it is absurd. It's none of it consistent. Why do you go into those details—the colour of his coat, the set of his pocket holes, and even what was painted on the wall of the ballroom?"

"Because I've seen that. Some of it I can't see, but I can see that and I have put it in."

Mrs. Fielding waved aside this explanation.

"And then the names! I don't believe he, the murderer, was named Philip."

"I didn't say he was a murderer, Grace. And as for the name, I don't know—yes, I did alter that. I like to call him Philip."

"Aren't you rather betraying yourself?"

"In what way betraying myself, Grace? Everyone betrays himself in his work, You can't keep it out—yourself I mean—— Of course, this is only the first rough draft of the story; I expect I shall alter it a good deal. But don't you like it?"

"Like it," she exclaimed. "Of course, it's all rubbish, and you could have said it in such few words. He married a woman for her money."

"There's a lot more in it than that, Grace. I wish you hadn't interrupted me just as I got to Barbara."

"Is Barbara so important?"

"Why, yes, of course; she was the reason for it all, the whole tragedy."

Mrs. Fielding rose and put the back of her hand to her mouth, a gesture as if she struck her lips. Why didn't he say Angela instead of Barbara? The whole device was so transparent. He must think her an utter fool. She looked down at him and spoke, her voice muffled against the back of her own hand.

"It's getting late. I think I'll go to bed."

"You don't want to hear any more, then?" he asked.

"Not to-night. I'm not sure, Philip, that it isn't all dangerous."

She did not know what made her say that; it seemed to her that she was speaking more to herself than to him. "I mean, we ought not to let these dead people get hold of us like this. There's peril in it, isn't there? We should never have come to this house. It might make one do things." She ventured a glance at him.

He smiled, shook his head.

"Oh, I don't go so far as that—hypnotism, hallucination—all the hundred and one names there are for it. No, I don't believe that. Besides, what did they do? I can't find out."

She said, trying to probe not only him but herself: "Why are we interested? Why do we care? Why are we going over all this old ground? It must be that the atmosphere of the house has got hold of us, Philip, and we ought to get away."

"Get away to what?" he asked; and she winced before the bleakness in his voice. "We haven't got a home, you know. Only a flat in London, and I don't feel that I could take up the old life."

"Don't you, Philip?" Her words were broken with an infinite regret. "But what about the Italian trip? You said you'd take me away."

"So I will, but I don't know why—Italy? We might meet him there—Vavasour, I mean. He was in Italy. I dare say that is where he learned how to——" Philip Fielding broke off his sentence so completely that it seemed to her as if he bit a word on his tongue.

"Learned to—what?" she challenged.

"Oh, I don't know. All his tricks."

"How to murder his wife," she suggested on a rising note.

"I don't say that." He fumbled with the manuscript, folded it into the heavy book with the rubbed leather binding. "I don't know that he did do that. Anyhow, he was never found out."

"Perhaps you'll find him out, Philip."

She moved slowly to the door. It suddenly seemed impossible for her to go up those dark stairs, lined with those heavy, blackened portraits in the tarnished frames; to pass down the ill-lit corridor and enter the bedroom—the bed with the needlework curtains, with the small modern medicine chest in which she kept the liquid that she had taken from her husband's dispatch case... prussic acid....

"Don't ever read me any more, Philip," she implored hurriedly. "I don't want to hear it. I'm afraid the story will begin to haunt me. Leave me alone. It's all nonsense, really. We don't even know that these people actually existed."

"But I thought you saw her tombstone to-day, Grace."

"That might have been another woman. I don't know—I don't want to think of it."

He rose, and again she stared at him. She had the impression that she had received so forcibly on the first night they had come to Medlar's Farm—that he was of gigantic stature and, moreover, entirely alien to herself.

"Possession, perhaps," she murmured, and he asked her what was the word that she had spoken so low, but she shook her head several times, as if weary of all subterfuge. She sank into her chair again.

"Read some more, Philip. I've changed my mind, I can't go to bed just yet." She dropped into her chair with a certain violence, as if she had been thrown; he was, half reluctantly, opening the book that contained the manuscript.

"What did they know of poisons in those days?" she asked, shading her eyes with the back of her thin hand.

"Oh, a great deal, I expect. It was so easy to get hold of, too——"

"You know a great deal, too, don't you, Philip? I remember you read it up once, with that man Bates——"

"Bates? Oh yes—he was very keen—about La Croix and La Voison and those people——"

"What did they use—cyanide of potassium?"

"I suppose so." He seemed surprised by her use of this word. "Prussic acid."

"Yes. It's marvellous what it will do, isn't it? Colourless, odourless, tasteless—I believe that you could use it in a syringe—a few puffs down your throat——"

"I never thought of it—I suppose you could. Pretty ghastly, eh? But Vavasour couldn't have used that way—they weren't known—sprays, I mean, then. I don't even know if he could have got hold of prussic acid——"

"Go on with the story——"

Philip Fielding began to read again.

*   *   *

" 'I should not care to stay here,' he admitted 'and there is little danger that I shall do so. I do not think that my uncle is very pleased to see me at Vavasour Hall.'

" 'You will go away again?' and desolation, like a veil, fell over her small, fine features.

"He did not answer, but continued to smile, as if he noticed neither her nor her distress.

"To describe him would be to give a false impression, I know, of his appearance. I have not yet completely seen him. His hair was reddish and grew strong and thickly, it was harsh in texture. His features, noble in themselves, seemed a mirror for gay, passionate, and strange thoughts which continually changed.

"That night there was a great snow-storm. All the north was muffled and white. There seemed no longer earth nor sky, flakes falling close and steady across the heavy grey buildings closed in the horizon so that one might not see much farther than one's own outstretched hand and brought hallucinations to those who continued to gaze at them; a man lost on the moors that night saw about him the likenesses of friends dead forty years and more.

"The complete stillness, the old furniture and the old boards that gave creaks that could be distinctly heard. Neither Philip nor Susanna could return to their homes that night. They slept for the first time under the same roof. He was woven into all her dreams like a thread of gold and scarlet.

"They met again in the morning, when he showed her some of his treasures; a casket of shells, some branches of coral, which he declared he had snatched from the hands of the sirens themselves, a necklace of thin gold coins like the last leaves of autumn. A fan, painted with a blue landscape; all these things looked strange in the cold light reflected from the snow without.

"The young woman was enchanted.

"She had her way like those under a spell often do. When the storm abated and the roads were passable her father drove over in a coach and four to Vavasour Hall and put his case before Philip's uncle; in brief, he offered the hand of his delicate heiress, and all her plumbago and coal mines, to the penniless Philip.

"The old Vavasour, I think, mocked a little, talked of women and fools and caprice, and asked what they knew of Philip who had been abroad so long and was by some accounts no better than a rogue, yet did not say from where had come these tales so disgraceful to his own blood, and in the end, yet not without a touch of malice, said: 'That if the lady would, she must.... No doubt Philip, for all he was such a vagabond, would be willing to pouch the money and settle down, but they must remember that the young man had nothing.'

"That point was emphasised. He stood three or four away from the succession to the Vavasour estates. His little portion he had long since squandered. The devil alone knew how he lived—perhaps on charity—he was no lover of work.

" 'I dare swear,' laughed old Vavasour, 'that when he gets in those strange foreign cities, he begs his way a little. He comes begging to me, at least, and a spendthrift he is beyond cavil. One who has never achieved anything, and has no ambition or endeavour in him, and has, too, if I now him, an obdurate, a savage heart—but if your daughter——'

" 'My daughter thinks he has all the qualities she admires. I, at least, have enough land for both. He will not want, Vavasour, with what I can give him.'

"The other man was amazed to hear Oldmixon thus plead his daughter's cause.

" 'You must,' he said good-humouredly, 'be bewitched to wish such a one for your son-in-law. But what is to be will be. It is a piece of good fortune—ridding me of the rogue. I'll tell him to get to work on his wooing.'

"So Philip Vavsour was told by his uncle of his great good fortune. How he might become master of the woman in the north, and of all her possessions, and how she was fair enough and young, and of good repute and, more important, weak and wilful, as her obstinate choosing of a scoundrel like himself showed, and therefore might, in the future, be easily overcome and managed. But Philip received this news sullenly; he was never one to care about money and possessions, nor to desire to stay long in one place. Besides, he had just seen Barbara."

*   *   *

Mrs. Fielding impatiently interrupted. Her silence and, apparently, her absorption in the story had been so complete that her sudden voice startled him, so that the manuscript slid from his hands.

"Don't you see,' she said contemptuously, "that it is simply our own story you are dwelling on?"

He repeated stupidly: "Our own story?"

"Yes," she said, "that's why I stopped you when you came to Barbara. Angela it should have been."

She left the room, fumbling out into the dark.

*   *   *

Philip Fielding followed his wife, as if he had been brought sharply back from his ghost world to a realisation of her distress.

"You must not think that for a moment, Grace. Why, the case is utterly different—his own experience is the last thing that a writer like myself draws on——"

He spoke gently, almost affectionately, to his wife as she paused by the newel post of the short, dark stairway.

"I'm going back into the library for a little, It isn't really late, and I want to see if I can get any more of the story. I'm beginning to think you're right. What I've written is rubbish, especially the snow-storm."

"No, that's quite true," she broke in quickly. "Can't you feel how cold the house is now—June, why, it's ridiculous, I'm sure the snow is thick outside."

He looked sharply at her, and the pity in his tone deepened as he laid his hand on her arm.

"You mustn't worry yourself about these things, Grace. I'm afraid it is bad for you—being here. I'd no idea you had so much imagination. You usually despise poor fancies. Are you sure you don't mind going upstairs alone?" She shook her head, and he continued: "You know I'd never have asked you to stay if you hadn't been so sure you don't mind."

The little flame of the night-lamp that she carried upstairs with her was between them. It clearly picked his features out from the surrounding dark; she moved it as if she did not wish to see his face just then, and slowly proceeded up the stars.

He called after her: "In that dark green dress you make me think of Susanna Vavasour herself."

Mrs. Fielding asked, turning to glance down over her shoulder: "How do you know she wore a dark green dress?"

"Well, I don't, really. I may have made it up or read it somewhere. Why does it surprise you?"

"Well, because I thought so too." She went on quickly up the stairs without waiting for him to reply. When she reached the top, she peered down over the balusters and saw that the hall was empty. He had, then, returned to the library and shut himself in, with what he termed his "poor fancies."

How could he be so tactless or so cruel? He had denied that she was the prototype of the woman in the story, yet said she reminded him of Susanna Vavasour.

His fancies, or those of another? Those, for instance, of the dead murderer? She held her lamp high, and glanced over the heavy portraits on the upper wall, pictures placed so high that all Mrs. Mace's housewifely care had not sufficed to keep them free of dust, even of cobwebs. Her light was reflected in the highly varnished surfaces of the dark canvases.

She noticed now what she had not observed before, that they were all of men. one of them, no doubt, was the creature whom her husband had named Philip Vavasour—the murderer, the justified murderer, who had disposed of the jealous woman who tormented him. Disposed of her, destroyed her, for the sake of Barbara.

Which was he, did anybody know?

Mrs. Fielding thought that all these masculine visages were repellent, that there was a slight distortion over each crudely delineated face. But she was beginning to imagine a slight distortion over everything, as if all the objects in the world had been slightly shaken out of place.

One of these painted figures wore a curious sage-green cloak bound with black, and carried, thrust into the folds of the breast, a stiff posy of unnatural looking, dim white flowers stained by tarnished red. The features were of a livid paleness, and Mrs. Fielding pondered as to whether or no this was a living creature or a dead body painted in grave-clothes.

She turned into her own room and lit the larger lamp which stood ready on the table by the bed.

Not afraid, not afraid of anything. So she assured herself. Why, she had never been afraid of the house nor of any phantoms there might be in it, and now her mood of fear of her husband had changed. She no longer dreaded him. She thought she had a guide and comforter, the prim-faced woman in the dark green dress like her own.

She thoughtfully stood by one of the posts of the narrow bed. With an idle finger she traced the design of bursting fruit and folded flower on the harsh twill where the thread, flourished there long ago by dead hands, was beginning to wear away.

She was endeavouring, through the slight and not disagreeable confusion that had fallen on her senses, which was like the first stage of the inhalation of a powerful drug, to trace out, with a cool logic, the most probable course that her husband would take.

Angela, no doubt, had come over in desperation, to urge on him some immediate action. When he discovered that the supposed poison was not efficacious—he might have discovered that already, for all she knew—very likely she had already drunk the water with which she had filled the bottle in his dispatch case.

When he had discovered that, what would he do? Procure some more prussic acid? How easy it would be for him to take her out one morning, driving the car himself She saw it all, the car, a picnic basket behind, Mrs. Mace smiling farewell from the steps, asking them if they'd forgotten the thermos and rugs, telling them the beauty spots they were to be sure not to miss.... No, that would not do. It must not be a picnic. He would tell the housekeeper that his wife had suddenly decided to leave. Had he not prepared the way for such a statement? He would say he was driving her to the station. There were many most lonely places where he could quite easily murder her; he had had many opportunities, on his lonely walks, of finding such a spot.

He could sink her body in a lonely tarn, or bury it in the dark woods, or even, with safety, leave it to bleach on some cold hill-side.

Yet she did not think he would do any of these things. She thought he would bring her back to Medlar's Farm, conceal her somewhere in the car and wait till everything was quiet at night, and then take her out and bury her in one of the cellars; or perhaps that was all nonsense, not the sort of plan that a murderer would think out at all. Perhaps he meant to give her another poison, one that acted slowly, like arsenic; perhaps he had the courage to watch her agony, summon a strange doctor from far away, see that she died before the doctor appeared. The whole done in order, an inquest perhaps, but no verdict, or an open verdict as in the case of Susanna Vavasour.

Well, it would not matter which way he chose, all of them would lead to freedom for him. Her anguish was due to that, not to the contemplation of her own tragedy, but to the prospects of his freedom.

That journey to Italy! He would go, no doubt, and Angela would be his companion.

She left the bed and walked round the room; then drew up suddenly before the small cupboard in which she had put the prussic acid. She did not know why she had not destroyed it. As she leant against the wall there she felt as if someone were soothing and comforting her, advising her.... She could not catch the sense of the counsel which was being given to her. Then she became incapable of clear reasoning, and odd, broken sentences fixed themselves stupidly in her mind.

That old tag[8]—"Hell hath no fury——" Then the sentence that her husband had spoken when she had told him about the queer sculpture which she had seen in Crompton Old Church: "The Devil Snar'd." There was some meaning there, and she was like one fumbling about in the dark to find the handle of a door. Then it seemed that she had discovered, grasped, and turned it, and light broke in on her slowly—a cold and awful light in which Hell stood clearly revealed.

She was so horrified by this lurid illumination which was worse than any darkness, that she tried, for the first time in her life, to pray, to honestly send up an appeal for help to some high and merciful Power. She could not do this, but she could check the horror which had been breaking on her—and she remained for a while mute and immobile, crouched below the corner in which was the small medicine cupboard.

She believed that she saw herself—or Susanna Vavasour, or her own evil angel—at least a creature in a dark green gown who seemed

---

[8] A short phrase or saying.

to hover, in the likeness of a cloud, a few feet above the floor—blot the ancient wall, and she held a muttered colluquy with this phantom.

"I ought to be sure that it is poison—first of all. I ought to be sure of that——"

"You are sure. Didn't you ask the chemist?"

"Yes, but I only described the stuff."

"You showed it to him, don't you remember? And he said that it was prussic acid—enough to kill three or four people."

"Did he? I forget. My mind has been so confused lately."

The shape, she thought, stooped down until it enveloped her like a miasma.

"You must not be confused about this. He brought that poison here to destroy you. Everything fits into that, doesn't it?"

"Yes."

"He has to wait an opportunity, and to get up his courage; that is why he is dwelling on that old story—just to find out how the other man did it——"

"Yes, yes, of course."

"But now the poison is in your possession——"

Mrs. Fielding made a violent move with her hands, and cast off the whispering shape that dissolved into silent shreds of darkness.

She remained seated on the floor in the corner. She heard her husband come up to his room and move about—to and fro, up and down. She crouched in stillness until there was silence from his chamber, and then she rose and stealthily bolted the door between their rooms—but not for fear of him.

*   *   *

Mrs. Fielding came down late the next morning.

Her husband asked her with anxious solicitude why she had not allowed him to send her breakfast up to her room. She replied that she had no appetite for any food. Then, seeing his concern at her distress, she made an effort to conceal this, and talked for a while of indifferent matters. But the pretence would not last. She rapidly said, with an uneven shrill note in her voice:

"I did not sleep well last night. Those draughts are no use any more. I must really have something stronger."

"I was reading late too; all that old stuff we were talking of down here," he replied with regret.

"No, no; it was not that at all. That quite went out of my mind. It was something I was reading just before I went to sleep. About a man," she hurried on, "who was practising the power of the human eye, as they used to call it. He practised on toads. He used to kill them by staring at them. Just get them somewhere where they could not move and gaze at them until they died. Then one day he got a toad which seemed to suspect his designs, for it made the most frantic efforts to escape. But at last, finding itself cornered, it turned and began to stare at him, and he found that he couldn't look away, that all his own power had gone. The toad, helpless, continued to stare at him. It was cornered, mind you, Philip, you mustn't forget that, and it kept on staring at him, and in the morning they found him dead on the floor of his laboratory. Don't you think that is a horrible story?"

"It is a ridiculous one," said Philip Fielding rather uneasily. "If the man was dead in the morning, how did anybody know that the toad had stared him to death?"

"It doesn't matter in the least," she muttered, "whether it's possible or not. It's the idea of the thing." Then suddenly throwing back her dark head, she asked him a question that utterly surprised him: "Where is Angela staying? I want to go to see her."

"Why, Grace, I think it would be the most absolute mistake."

"I must see her, Philip. I really must."

He hesitated before the insistency, almost the appeal, in her voice.

"Do you really feel you want to see Angela? Feel kindly enough towards her for that? No! Don't do it, Grace. Besides, I expect she's left the lakes."

"I'm not going to make a scene," said Mrs. Fielding quietly.

"She's not the least what you think she is."

"I don't want to quarrel with Angela. You must see that. I've avoided plenty of chances of doing that."

"That's true," he agreed.

"Perhaps," she hurried on, in a dull flat tone, "I've relented, I've seen what a monstrous, crazy, stupid thing I'm doing. Don't you think that might happen, Philip?"

"I don't now how to take you this morning, Grace."

"Don't fence with me. It's not like you to fence with me. You know perfectly well you don't care for me any more, but you're still longing for Angela. You know what she's feeling about it too. Well then, I don't say I am not going to set you free. There might be a chance if you let me go and see her."

The eager expectancy in his look was as unmistakable as it was hateful to Mrs. Fielding. She went on, talking rapidly without much sense of what she was saying, but merely to put a barrier of words between herself and the possibility of violent action.

"Don't you think that the moment has come to be sensible? Angela and I might understand each other, after all. Of course, I was very rude to her the other day. I don't want to leave it like that. It's childish, don't you see? Tell me where she is, Philip."

He was silent, with the air of one trying to carefully choose words in a moment of excitement. This gave her further courage.

"You can trust me not to make a scene, can't you? In a public place. I'm past all that, too exhausted."

"Yes, yes, Grace. I wasn't thinking of that, but whether it's wise, whether we ought not to put it out of our minds altogether."

"But you know that we haven't. You're always thinking of Angela, and so am I. She might really as well be here, living with us."

"You're wrong," he quickly replied, but it seemed to his wife without conviction. "I wish you could understand me, Grace. I hoped that you did. No doubt you think I am letting it all go by default. We discussed everything so frankly in London, and I felt I couldn't go over it any more. I hope everything will be all right without that."

To her these broken, rather stiff sentences were only so many evasions. She continued to deliberately deceive him, as she believed he was deliberately deceiving her.

"I'm trying to get it all on to a better level, don't you see? There are some things I'd like to talk over with Angela. One ought to respect Angela, after all, don't you think?"

It was very strange, she thought, that he could accept her strange grin as a smile. He appeared to do so, and even touched her arm affectionately.

"Yes, yes," he agreed earnestly. "I am so thankful to hear you say that. I expect Angela must seem to you just a greedy little hussy, mean and hateful. She is not, indeed she is not. I'd like you to know it. I'd even like Angela and you to be friends. It's possible, isn't it?"

She turned away to hide her face, for she knew by now that her grin must be frightful. She had heard before that men indulged in this most stupid of delusions—that of supposing that two jealous women could, under any circumstances, become friends or admire each other. How was it possible that he, Philip, supposed to be so subtle and sensitive, could be thus thick-witted? His incredible stupidity suited her purpose.

"Tell me where Angela is, and I will get Hicks to drive me over. I suppose one can get there and back quite easily in an afternoon? I dare say we can find many points in common, and might clear some things up."

At that he took an old envelope from his pocket and wrote on it an address, the name of a village and a hotel, near one of the lakes, not fifteen miles away.

"I don't know if she's still there," he said doubtfully. "If you like to try, if you think it's any use——"

She interpreted his keen and wistful look as meaning: "Are you, after all, going to put us out of our misery? Are you going to give us our freedom?" But these were not the words he said. Taking hold of her wrist, he awkwardly got out:

"I wish you didn't think I was such a cad, Grace. I always feel you do, even when you are trying to be pleasant. I ought to explain, but aren't explanations—painful? It wasn't a question of leaving you for somebody else, or of preferring somebody to you. I know that would be quite unforgivable. It was just a feeling that we—our connection, whatever it meant, was dead, dead to you as well as me. And that we ought, each of us, to try and make something fresh. Don't you see, our marriage had gone quite decayed and corrupt about us, and was poisoning us. I felt we ought to get away, for your sake as well as mine. Angela was my way of escape."

"Do you still feel that?"

"No, no." He shook his head again, but his words brought no conviction to her. "I don't say I do. Everything's been different since we've been in this house. As I said before, that life in London was stifling. Just a dead weight and trivialities. But here I've found what really matters."

"Your story?" she asked. "The story of your murderer?"

He did not flinch, even at this, which should, she knew, have stabbed him on the raw. She quailed before his courage. Nervous and sensitive as he seemed, he must have the steel nerve, the unrelenting purpose, of the accomplished criminal.

"Poor Philip Vavasour," was all he said. "I've written some more of that tale. I'd like to read it to you when you come back. I'm trying to see that it was not all dun and horrible. The dark side of love, I thought it at first. But now I'm getting through. I can't say I see more, but there is a greater light. I think I can redeem them yet."

"What was Barbara like?" Is there a picture of her anywhere?"

"No, I don't think so. I haven't bothered much about Barbara."

"Was she like Angela?" asked Mrs. Fielding.

He looked at her in what seemed genuine surprise.

"Angela and Barbara! Why, I never thought of them together. I told you so before——"

He looked at her in a peering sort of way.

"What have you got in your head, Grace? You seem to me to have been rather unlike yourself lately, as if you're feeling after something. What is it? You've told me again and again that the old house and the old story are not getting on your nerves."

"I don't know."

He took her by the arm and stared at her with considerable appeal. "I wish I could get you where I am, Grace. I wish we could see eye to eye. Just the same distance, as it were, and the same horizon."

"What do you want me to see?" she asked. She thought of her own future grave in the deserted cellars of Medlar's Farm. No doubt that was the focus of his intense vision.

"I wish we weren't all so afraid of words," he said, almost suddenly. "This terror of being emotional and melodramatic; and if one's a trained writer it's worse. One's terrified of falling into the tricks of the trade. Words have been used too often, haven't they? Clipped and defaced like a base coinage."

"Still," she urged, "you're usually glib enough, Philip. Tell me before I go to see Angela what it is you want me to see eye to eye with you. Look, I am perfectly calm."

"I suppose," replied Philip Fielding quietly, "that what I've realised and what I'd like you to realise, dear, is that when it's all gone beyond chance of recovery, all the dreams, the hopes, the expectations gone, there's still enough left to make it worth while going on."

"That sounds like a riddle to me. Unless you just mean that we're growing old." Her voice rose high and shrill on the last words. She steadied herself and added: "See Hicks for me, will you, and order the car."

*　　　*　　　*

Mrs. Fielding had always been afraid of nature. She relished a landscape in a picture or seen from a distance or through a window, but like so many town-bred people she had a terror of lonely fields, lonely roads, of solitary woods, she would not have gone on foot after dark two miles away from a human habitation. She had never tried to analyse these fears. She merely avoided what she rather vaguely called "the country." But as the car took her along solitary by-ways which led to the village where Angela was now staying, all these old dreads and fears dating back to her early childhood returned to her, and she connected them with her present tragedy.

The road dipped past a lake, ran up a hill, skirted a belt of woods, showed glimpses here and there of distant vales and waters, and all was awful to Grace Fielding. She wondered how anyone could have thought of nature as benevolent or gracious, as the kindly mother. Nature seemed instead a frightful destructive force, against whom long years of civilisation had scarce the might to raise barriers.

Every building that man had erected, every road he had laid down, every field he had hedged, every tree he had felled, seemed to Mrs. Fielding's overwrought mind like another feeble effort to thrust back and to hold at bay this mighty and malevolent power that dwelt in all lonely places; the waters of the lake were dark with the blackness of corruption, there was a livid carrion look about the bare sides of the distant hills where the dead heather, the colour of old blood, clung like patches of decay; she hated the woods in which no pleasant green plant grew and where the light only fell in bleached sparkles between the close trunks, and yet she was almost impelled to stop the car and wander away into those lonesome depths.

In the stretch of dale land, where there was no habitation in sight, they came to a gate in a stone wall. A ragged boy opened it for them. She saw a shelter made of sacking, dry heather, and boughs against the wall. The boy seemed delighted with the silver she gave him, and explained that the gate was shut because of the sheep. She thought his withered face repellent, and the thought of his vigil there, in that great loneliness, made her shudder.

"He must be by himself for hours, for the sake of a few pence— for how often do cars pass here. And what use is money to him in such a wilderness?"

Then, as someone drowning rises for the last time, and glimpses in a swirl of radiance the final gleam of day, she thought: "It is all right, really. It is only I who am infected." But she could not throw off this infection. "There must be something most horribly amiss with me, that I can see nothing lovely or pleasant anywhere." She looked down at her long hand in the lap of her green tweed dress, at the rings and bracelets that Philip had given her, that now seemed to hang so slackly on her lean flesh, and again she thought of her bones which might soon be rotting in the cellars of Medlar's Farm as the bones of Susanna Vavasour were rotting in Crompton Old Church.

Mrs. Fielding was very tired when she reached the quiet but fashionable hotel where Angela was staying. She felt her limbs stiff when she descended from the car, an odd lightness in her head. Perhaps she had undertaken more than she could do, but her spirit, roused at her need, made a strong clutch on her sick body, and sent her into the hall, asking for Angela.

The actress was still there, though she was leaving that afternoon. Mrs. Fielding sent up her name, and went into the parlour which was arranged with studied unsophistication. Blue china on racks, sepia water colours of the lakes, and old pieces of dark polished furniture, all very clean yet smelling faintly of decay.

Mrs. Fielding approached the large coal fire, surprised to discover how cold were her hands and feet.

Angela came down almost at once. Mrs. Fielding was encouraged by seeing that she had lost her air of maddening self-confidence, and appeared agitated, almost alarmed. But Mrs. Fielding was also exasperated by observing that her rival's beauty, which had been so in eclipse on the day of her visit to Medlar's Farm, was now vivid with a feverish brilliance, lips moist and red, her cheeks glowing as if she had been walking in the wind and rain, and her eyes shining with a lustre which did not seem to be all reflected light, but to come from some inner passion.

"Did you want to see me?"

Mrs. Fielding nodded. The two women sat down, one either side of the fire. Mrs. Fielding was facing the window, the light of which made an aureole of gleaming threads on Angela's untidy hair. In this window hung a wire basket full of fleshy, pink, hothouse flowers and moist trailing ferns. Beyond she could see a square of lawn sodden from the late rain. A gardener was placidly at work, snipping off the soaked, bruised heads of the dead roses.

"Angela, I'm glad you haven't gone. I wanted to see you."

The other woman turned, on the defensive. Mrs. Fielding noted the firm whiteness of her throat where the yellow woollen bodice was open, observed the rounded curves of her arms in the tight clinging sleeves as they rested on the leathern sides of the chair, and thought of Philip.

"I don't see what there can be to say," said Angela with her usual frankness, but not with her usual insolence. "I suppose you know that Philip sent me away?"

Mrs. Fielding felt no triumph at this, as she would have felt a few weeks ago. She believed it a deliberate lie, part of a deliberate scheme.

"Did he?" she said in a flat voice. "I don't see that that makes much difference; it's all got rather ridiculous. I thought that you and I —two women—might clear it up a little. Philip gets involved with words. We ought not to hate each other, you know, Angela."

"But we do," smiled the other woman. "Won't you have some coffee? You look fagged out. It's a lonely drive, I know; it gets on one's nerves. Of course if you're going to be decent, I shall be awfully grateful."

"By decent, you mean, am I going to allow, after all, the divorce?"

"I suppose I do mean that," said Angela. Mrs. Fielding noticed that she was shivering.

"I wonder what you see in Philip?" asked Philip's wife.

"I wish I could tell you. It's not fun for me, I assure you. It's tragic. It's simply killing me, the whole affair. I couldn't tell you what it is, whether it's just the old stuff, love at first sight, soul-mate, and all the rest."

"Men's second wives, when they're successful, are nearly always their soul-mates, and they're nearly always twenty years younger and thirty years more beautiful than the first wife."

"Well, you can put it like that," said Angela. "If you haven't come to tell me you're setting him free, I don't know why you have come. It can't be very pleasant for you, seeing me."

Mrs. Fielding thought: "If she knew the real reason for my coming, she'd think I was mad. I dare say she'd have me locked up or, if she knows what he's going to do, she wouldn't think me mad, but she'd warn him. He would be very quick about it. It would happen, perhaps, as soon as I returned to Medlar's Farm."

She put her fingers to her throat, and began plucking at the flesh there, as if trying in advance what it would feel like to have the life strangled out of her.

Angela rang the bell and ordered coffee.

"I haven't got a private sitting-room, but we shall be absolutely quiet here. There's only one or two people staying in the hotel, and they've gone off on some expedition. I ought to tell you that Philip didn't really know I was coming up to that awful place where you've taken him."

"Where he's taken me."

"Well, anyhow, I suppose I ought to let you know that. He didn't. It was quite my own idea. I suppose you will think it was quite shameless of me, but if I hadn't come you would have thought I was a coward, wouldn't you?"

"No, Angela," smiled Mrs. Fielding, "I should never think you were a coward."

"Well, I've tried to be frank. I don't see that what I did was so dreadful. I've tried to understand your point of view too."

"Have you, Angela?" I never thought of that."

"Oh, I have, indeed. One has to put up a sort of self-defence. One gets hard when one feels strongly, you know. It's all pretty sickening, and I'm sure you thought I was just out for money, and his position. But it wasn't that."

"I don't care what it was," said Mrs. Fielding. "I haven't come to talk about that, and haven't got very much strength to talk about anything. I think they're coming with the coffee."

She leant back in her chair, and Angela relaxed her attitude into one of indifference. The maid brought in the coffee service.

When they were alone again both the women drank eagerly.

Mrs. Fielding fastened her gaze on the basket of frail, pink, fleshy-looking flowers trembling in the window-place, and on the figure of the man beyond walking round the verge of the damp grass, snipping at the sodden roses.

"Tell me what it's all about," urged Angela. She turned her large, slightly protuberant, brilliant eyes towards Mrs. Fielding, and added: "You poor thing, you really do look worn out. Whatever made you go to that horrible place? It seemed like a charnel-house to me. I know you think I'm an utter beast, but I have been frank, haven't I? What is the use of you and Philip just dragging on? You are still young, and there are heaps of other men in the world. I dare say that sounds vulgar, but we ought to be past pretences."

Angela had never before spoken with so much kindness and good feeling towards her victim, but this increased Mrs. Fielding's suspicion.

Angela was, then, an accomplice. Her business was to soothe, to placate. No doubt Philip had told her she had made a mistake in coming to Medlar's Farm; no doubt, she was trying, by a submissive behaviour, to-day to gloss over that mistake.

Mrs. Fielding drank another cup of coffee, and steadied herself not to swerve from the resolution which had brought her on this journey. She saw just one chance, for herself, for Philip, and even for Angela.

"It's not all over," she said rapidly. "I suppose you know that? It may seem very smooth, on the surface, I mean, but when he and I went away—I suppose it stopped the scandal—but that's not everything."

"I suppose you mean that though he left me he hasn't come back to you, not really?"

Mrs. Fielding did not directly answer this. She drank some more coffee, and warmed her hands and stared again at the basket of wax-like flowers in the window, before she answered.

"I mean that what you did isn't over, it's—like throwing a stone in a pond—the ripples go out and on for quite a long time. If you really want to efface yourself out of Philip's life——"

"But I don't," interrupted Angela. "Why do you suppose I came over to Medlar's Farm the other day? I couldn't believe that you would still want to keep him."

"Don't let's go over that, please. I'm sure I read somewhere that women can discuss these things, nowadays, quite coolly. There's all sorts of ways, aren't there, of being matter-of-fact, on these matters?" She remembered her husband's words: "One must not be melodramatic or emotional." "And I believe if one if really clever and smart and up-to-date, like you are, Angela, one can talk about the changing about one's husband or one's lover without showing any feeling at all."

"I have never been able to do it," muttered Angela, "and I must say it isn't very easy now. What have you come for? If you're still standing firm——if you won't give him the divorce——"

"I won't," said Mrs. Fielding, "I won't, I won't." She checked herself, feeling that the reiteration of the word would drive her out of control and added hastily:

"I've come to appeal to you to let go. That's what I want, Angela. I want you to write to him and tell him that you have really done with him. I want you to go away on that tour to Africa, India, Canada, I don't care where. I want you to, if possible, marry someone else. To cut right out of his life." She added on a sunken note: "That's the only way to save us."

Without reflecting a second Angela said: "I won't do it."

"You're convinced then, he still cares for you?"

"Of course. Poor Philip, he's trying to do his duty by you. I dare say he's sorry for you, but you must see for yourself——"

"Never mind what I see for myself," interrupted Mrs. Fielding. "It doesn't do to talk too much of what I see for myself." Repeating this again, she added: "It's because of what I see for myself I'm here."

"You're not very coherent," said Angela. "If you've come to me asking for any sacrifice or renunciation, I simply can't give it. Philip left me of his own free will. He chose between us. That sounds silly and simple, doesn't it? But he chose you, and you've got him. You must make the best of it. If you're driving him crazy, or he's driving you crazy, that's no affair of mine. I'm not leaving England, and I'm not marrying anybody else. If he ever gets sick of you, I shall be there."

"That's a funny way to put it," sighed Mrs. Fielding, rising. Angela thought she had never looked so tall. She had certainly grown very much thinner during her residence at Medlar's Farm. "I thought you didn't want him unless you could marry him."

"It depends," declared Angela, with her devastating frankness, "how long you can hang on. I might get tired. I might take him without marriage. I don't know! I'm still hoping you'll change your mind and give us the divorce."

There was a large tropical plant with a single crimson flower on the mantelpiece. Mrs. Fielding looked past this at her reflection in the mirror beyond, and saw the red bloom like a blot against her thin throat. Looking into her own eyes she said:

"Of course—there's just one other prospect. I might die, you know, and then you could marry him, couldn't you? Without any more trouble at all."

"I hadn't thought of that. One doesn't, somehow!"

Mrs. Fielding's lips formed the word "Liar." Aloud she said:

"Something horrible will happen if you don't do this, Angela. Something you've not thought of at all, but that I know of. Won't you change your mind? You've got Philip on a sort of chain. If you would just snap it——"

"I'm not going to. You're mad to ask it. Even if I were to make you a promise like that, I shouldn't keep it. You're the one who ought to give way, and you know it. Of course, something dreadful may happen if you go on living in that horrible place. One or both of you will go mad, I suppose that's what you mean. It's ghastly for Philip. A sacrifice to his duty. I don't know how he can do it."

Mrs. Fielding continued to stare at her livid reflection in the mirror.

"Put it, then, for Philip's sake," she said; "say, to save Philip, you give him up. If you were to make it quite definite that he's nothing whatever to hope from you, everything would be different. He'd leave Medlar's Farm and go away. Perhaps I'd let him go away alone. He'd forget all about it. Everything would be, in time, like it used to be."

Angela shook her tousled head.

"No, it wouldn't. We can't forget each other. You ought to understand that. It's no good saying it's for Philip's sake. It's just your own jealousy speaking. I'm jealous, too, but it isn't out of jealousy I'm acting. It's because I know it would be of no use."

Mrs. Fielding moved from the mirror and picked up her handbag and her gloves from the pretty chintz covered chair.

"That sounds final. Very well, Angela, I've made an appeal, and you've refused. You'll take the consequences. Perhaps they won't be quite what you think they will."

"That sounds like a threat."

Angela's voice was faint, as if the struggle had been too much for her. It was the first time that Mrs. Fielding had observed her display any signs of weakness.

"You can take it like a threat if you like. Remember, afterwards, that I did give you this chance."

"I don't know what you're talking about," said Angela rather wildly. "But you look really awful. I shall write to Philip and tell him that he ought to have you looked after. I don't think you're quite responsible for what you're saying or doing."

Mrs. Fielding recoiled.

"Oh, I give you that impression, do I?"

"You do, rather. I say, you are all right, aren't you?"

Mrs. Fielding did not answer. She was pulling on her gloves, slowly, finger by finger. As if in self-defence and with an effort to be generous, Angela continued:

"After all, you ought to have all the winning cards, you know. You've got him there, day and night. You ought to be able to stand up for yourself and get him back if it's possible at all. I won't come again. I'll promise you that. Of course, I shall write, but you could intercept the letters, couldn't you? You see, you've got all the chances I haven't. I wish you wouldn't look so ghastly. I wish we could settle it all in a decent manner."

"That's wishing we'd both been different sorts of women. I don't think it's the kind of thing you can settle in a decent manner. You'll soon know how it's going to be settled, and then perhaps you'll wish——"

She broke off and pulled open her handbag, and snatched out her handkerchief and passed it rapidly across her face.

Angela said:

"I don't want to be a brute. Won't you stay here and have some food? If you hate to be in the same place where I am, there's another hotel a little farther up the village. Quite a decent place."

"How fond you are of that word decent," smiled Mrs. Fielding. "What quite does it mean, nowadays, I wonder?"

*   *   *

On the return journey Mrs. Fielding stopped the car at the edge of the wood that bordered the lake with a lonely island in the centre.

When she had passed that group of trees before they had repelled her—they repelled her still, but lured her, too; she was bound to enter and walk under the cold, dark shade.

The moment she left the car she felt that she had left a place of protection, was exposed to many hostile influences. She walked trembling over a carpet of ground ivy and small plants; the only ones which were known to her were daisies.

She saw the water twinkling cold in between the dark trunks; she believed that her companion was the shape of Susanna Vavasour.

She no longer tried to make credible explanations to herself about her conviction that this dead woman who had never left the earth had become her guide ever since she had come to Medlar's Farm; in the same way as Philip Vavasour was the guide of her husband.

But the shade in the tight green dress which matched the colour of the foliage no longer turned to her with the look of one trying to say something to her; what Susanna Vavasour had to say, Mrs. Fielding now knew....

She went to the edge of the lake, an irregular shaped piece of water which ran in and out the dark outlines of the hills. It was towards evening, the sky seemed both hollow and transparent, like a great glass bell, thought Mrs. Fielding.

She remembered a horrid experiment which she had once read of: a mouse and a scorpion were once set by some inquisitive man of science under a glass bell, where finally, after a dreadful duel, the timid beast killed the poisonous insect. The same story, of course, as that of the man and the toad. It was her story.

She looked at the island, on which grew three trees, and thought that if she could reach that she might find herself at peace and be able to die without doing that which she felt herself impelled to do.

But there was no boat. She wondered if anybody ever did go to the island. Salvation was always just out of reach.

She knew that it would be better for her if she could sink beneath the cold waters of the lake into an eternal oblivion. She could not choose.

A white shape floated in the shadow of the island, a solitary white swan. Everywhere she looked, every thought that came into her head held an omen. She touched the sedges that trembled in the water; an unutterable nostalgia and melancholy bowed her spirit and confused her mind in a rising miasma of horror.

"How odd," she said sullenly to herself, "that people should have thought that Susanna Vavasour was the victim. She must have been very clever—yet how did she contrive it, when he must have died first? Only I, who have known her since she was dead," added Mrs. Fielding, "really know her. To me she is not disguised."

She peered keenly round to see if she could discover the shape in the dark green dress passing between the close-set tree-trunks. She strained her ear to catch some whispered counsel or warning.

But the silence was as complete as it had been the day of her visit to the churchyard by Crompton Old Water. Only a little, low wind whispered over the water and stirred the leaves of the quiet trees.

Mrs. Fielding returned slowly to the car. Hicks looked rather curiously at her; he said something about a chilly evening, and getting home before the rain came… those clouds in the west would move up very quickly, he was sure. Mrs. Fielding had not noticed the clouds, but she noticed the word home, which had become lately, when applied to Medlar's Farm, most horrible.

Philip was waiting for her on the front doorstep. It was a long time since he had done that, but then, it was a long time since she had been to see Angela.

He helped her from the car, hoped she was not cold or tired. Mrs. Mace had a fine fire in the Tudor room. Grace had just escaped the rain, which was beginning to fall in large drops. He had been lonely without her, and had not been able to get on with his work. She smiled at him in return for all this solicitude. Anyone might have thought that they were happy. As he took her coat from her on the threshold, she thought:

"It is not so difficult to act and lie. I thought Angela so clever to-day, but, after all, I can do it too."

When she was in the easy chair by the fire, she told him in what she was sure was a natural tone:

"Angela is quite a dear. You were right, Philip. She is going back to London to-day. She is writing to you. I don't see why she shouldn't be, some day, all right."

"I'm glad," he answered abruptly. "Awfully glad, Grace. I won't ask what you mean by all right."

"No, please, don't. One must have time."

She looked at him from eyes swollen with fatigue.

"You're a very patient man, Philip. I'm learning to be patient too." And then, deliberately striking a false note, she added harshly: "What do they call it nowadays in the modern jargon? Sublimating the emotions, isn't it?"

But even at that he would not show vexation, and said nothing more about Angela. Of course there was only one explanation for his control... it would not have to last long.

Their meal was pleasant, Philip made himself agreeable on a dozen indifferent topics, and she was quite intelligent and charming about what she had seen on her journey to and from Angela's hotel. She said nothing, of course, of the woods where she had crossed the ground ivy and stood among the sedges, and the swan in the shadow; nor of the island with the three trees, or of her own sense of how much better it would have been for her to have slipped under the water of the lake—to have drowned herself as Susanna Vavasour's resting-place was to be drowned.

She wore her dark green dress which he had once said made her look like Susanna Vavasour, and afterwards they went into the library. He took up his manuscript and read her again more of the old story, prefacing it with this explanation, which he gave her hurriedly, as if he wished to avoid personal matters.

"Of course, Grace, all the old sayings are really most true. I mean about love and hatred being so close together, repulsion and attraction, all the ebb and flow of the same emotion."

"I know, I know," she said impatiently.

"Well, I don't want to be banal, Grace, but it's so clearly marked in this story. I don't know what I read you before, I've forgotten."

"So have I," said Mrs. Fielding. "It doesn't matter. Anything you've got—well, read it——"

"She married him; by sheer feminine tenacity she married him."

"I suppose you mean," said Grace, leaning towards the fire, "that he just wanted her money. That's the usual solution, isn't it?"

She was rather puzzled about this part of the story, for it did not fit in with her own. Philip had not married her for money; but—she remembered her own small capital, ridiculous of course, but it had helped him, and then what had she not done in sheer work and labour? Why, it would have cost him quite a lot of money for the services of housekeeper and secretary, a companion, a general slave. Well, if he hadn't married her for money he had married her for what he could get out of her, and he had had it out of her for years....

"Isn't that it?" she repeated. "He just married her for that."

"I don't know. He was a wild, adventuring spirit; he'd been all over the world without a ha'penny in his pouch."

"And then he comes home and marries a woman he doesn't care about and settles down. I suppose," said Mrs. Fielding, "he intended from the very first to make an end of her and go off again with her fortune on any journey—eh?"

Philip Fielding shook his head.

"That's too brutal and cold-blooded. That's not really human. I can't follow that at all. He was quite an honourable sort of man, not a born criminal. I don't believe people plan crimes of violence years ahead. They have to be exasperated, cornered, like he was."

"Well, he married her. That's enough, isn't it? Go on."

"Yes, and they lived for a while outside Hexham."

Philip Fielding was turning over the papers laying within the radius of his reading lamp.

"I've got some pictures of the place here. They've all got that ghastly bleak look of early steel engravings. But, of course, it was a human dwelling. It must have had its pleasant aspects."

"I don't see much pleasant aspect about any of the tale," smiled Mrs. Fielding. Then again she urged hurriedly, "Go on."

"They lived there and her father paid for their maintenance, until he, by a most unexpected series of deaths, just like any old melodrama—I can't make out how all these men perished, but they did, about five of them—he came into the succession. His kingdom, this estate, Vavasour Hall as it was, the very house where we sit now. He brought her home. Her fortune, then, was a matter of indifference to him. He had, on his own, all the money he wanted. There were, after three years of marriage, no children, and that was a source of deep vexation. In those days," added Philip Fielding, with what may have been studied carelessness, "of course, children were very important."

"I suppose they are, sometimes, now."

"Well, I suppose so, but I mean we don't lay all that stress on them people did then. It was a question of a man's name, almost of his honour. Philip Vavasour, lord of the Vavasour estates, was quite a different man from the vagabond who was wandering over Europe without a penny in his poke or a care in his mind."[9]

---

[9] Poke: a wallet or purse.

Philip Fielding paused, laid down his unlit pipe, and folded over the pile of papers.

"But I don't know," he added thoughtfully, "when he began to hate her."

"I think I do," said Mrs. Fielding, clasping her long fingers around her long knees. "It was when he first saw Barbara."

"No, I think it was before that. It was when he began to feel himself tied. He and this woman shut in this house. It is, of course, a horrible thing to live with someone whom you dislike and whom you can't get rid of. Dislike turns to hatred and hatred to murder. It's quite simple, really. She was none of your placid victims. She was a woman of character, of determination. She was, I think, in every way, save that of physical beauty, the superior of Barbara, who was the daughter of a yeoman farmer hereabouts. They were all, as I see it, quite frank one with another. When she first discovered that he was in love with Barbara, she probed the matter to the bottom. She was frightfully jealous, but she was prepared to endure an intrigue. They were common enough in those days. Women had to put up with them, and she had strong common sense. She found that Barbara and he were really infatuated, then she became alarmed. She faced him. She told him what she thought. And he said that it was true, that he would like to get rid of her and marry Barbara."

Philip Fielding looked at his wife beyond the radiance of the hand lamp. She shrank back against her chair and thought: "How can he? How can he tell me this story so like our own? Is it to warn me, to give me a chance of escape, or merely for the pleasure of tormenting me?"

Philip Fielding suddenly withdrew his glance, sighed, and dropped his head in his hands.

"I can't get any further than that," he said.

94

"It seems to me," muttered Mrs. Fielding, "far enough. He had no choice but to murder her. Have you not described that?" she asked, "the murder? Have you found out how it was done? He must have been clever, since there was an inquest but no verdict. He got away with it, didn't he? He had her buried. I suppose he married Barbara. Have you got all that?"

"I've got some of it, Grace. Why are you so interested? I thought you didn't care two straws about the old stuff. I've been wondering myself if it's a good story—if there's anything in it. I don't know—it puzzles me and weighs on me. Of course there is not only something but everything in atmosphere. It's coming to a place like this and exposing oneself to these old influences. It was stupid to do it, but I had to have a distraction."

"On her tomb," shivered Mrs. Fielding, "she has—'What I have done, I shall answer for——' or words to that effect. Does that give you any clue? Does that help?"

He shook his head.

"I went over to see that the other day, after what you told me. I couldn't decipher much, only those words and the names. I don't see anything in it. It may have been added later. The whole thing's a bundle of contradictions. What has she to answer for, poor soul? And yet I don't know. To provoke someone to murder you—I suppose it it pretty ghastly. Murdering a soul, isn't it? She got the martyr's crown and he hell fire, at least that would be the old belief. I think that that may have been it. She stayed here and provoked him to murder her, and when she was dead she knew what a ghastly thing she'd done. Of course he used to walk for years, be seen continually, he often had a nightcap on and a sage-green robe bound with black."

"That's the portrait on the stairs."

"Yes, I believe that's he, but there, again, one's baffled. I think the face has been repainted. That man has not red hair."

"Would his hair remain red when he was dead?"

Philip Fielding shook his head.

"I don't know. I haven't thought of it. Let me read you what I've written. If you're interested, I'd like to know what you think of it, if it sounds like sense."

*   *   *

"Philip Vavasour often used to meet Barbara by the tarn high up in the hills. It was covered with red lichen and supposed to be fathomless; leeches were to be found there, but no fish. Near by was a large boulder which was called the Wishing Stone. Philip and Barbara had often crossed hands over it according to the subscribed rites, and wished, but so far their desires had not come to fruition. There always seemed to be a little creeping wind in this spot, although it was shut in by the hills, being on a ledge between two heights. There were no trees about save one or two lone thorns which bore scant blossoms, few leaves, and no fruit. The ground was always wet and cold, for beneath the heather and moss ran untainted rivulets from the hilltop. To walk there was to have the feet wet and cold to the ankles, to kneel down there and press one's hand into the chill green was to have one's palm full of pure water.

"It was on an autumn day when the clouds were very low and dissolving now and then into mists which obscured all save the pool and the thorn trees that grew near it, and Barbara told Philip that her father was becoming discontented at her long visits to this lonely spot, and with her known infatuation for a man who could not marry her. She had spoken of this before, there never had been any subterfuge between them.

"This afternoon her tone was definite. She looked at him expectantly. He did not answer; he took off one of his heavy gauntlets with the long tassels and set his teeth in the palm. He was a very strong man and one on whom an inactive life was beginning to press hard. The tragedy of waste was beginning to master him, waste of strength, of time, of love, of life itself. She, looking enviously at his magnificence, thought of this, and her sharp regret was echoed in his mind. So it seemed to them that they felt time flowing away between them and taking with it all they valued, for they were neither of them of a character to relish the placid delights, if there be any, of old age.

"He said at length, looking down at the marks his teeth had left in the coarse leather:

" 'Susanna won't give way. I never begged for anything hard before, but I begged hard for this.'

"Barbara smiled at his simplicity.

" 'The harder you beg the greater your offence.'

" 'I know. But what was I to do? I've offered her back all her dowry. All her estate, every penny of it, and more besides, but still she just smiled and said: "No, no!" '

"The mist was closing up round them, moving in steady gusts down the hills, and Barbara pulled her grey woollen hood closer round her face.

" 'I can wait no longer,' she said. 'I shall go away. I shall marry another man.'

"The nearest thorn tree made a dark, sharp, crooked line against the encroaching mist. They both looked at it. It was the only definite object in a world of water and vapour.

" 'You must decide,' she said, and she sat down on the Wishing Stone and clasped her hands round her knees.

"He was very splendidly dressed, as one not afraid to flaunt his station, the highest in this wild country. He had lately taken a dislike to the red colour of his hair, and it was thickly pomaded in a fashion not common to the countryside, though necessary in town. This destroyed the natural hues of his face and gave his countenance a livid look. His strong tresses seemed to resist the flour and grease, and where the thick curls broke from the riband on to the blue coat Barbara could see the natural harsh auburn colour; his coat was gallooned with bullion and his laces were costly. He carried a small sword. There was broken moss and heather on his wet boots; he had no hat despite the dampness of the mist; there was thrown over his arm a long, dark, high-collared cloak, heavy with moisture. He stared into the vapours in a peering fashion, as if expecting somebody to step out of that approaching obscurity and challenge him.

" 'She fell down a short flight of stairs the other day,' he said. 'The heel came off her shoe. I could not go forward to help her. I thought that would have been the best way for all of us.'

"Barbara indifferently replied.

" 'I think she would be better dead. A sour, barren, jealous woman.'

" 'She would be better at rest,' he answered. 'She is so restless, Barbara. Up and down the house all day. Even at night she rises, takes a taper in her hand, and passes up and down the stairs and in and out of all the empty rooms. And when I ask her about it she has some shallow excuse—that she has remembered some disorder in the household linen, or is searching for a shift she has forgotten. Or wishes to see if the maids have properly performed their tasks.'

" 'Rest, she would never rest,' said Barbara, 'even if she were dead.'

" 'If she were dead I should not be afraid of her,' he smiled. 'I should marry you then, Barbara.'

" 'And take me to her house, to listen to her walking up and down all day and night?'

" 'Those tales have no credit with me. I never could see that if you had sufficient courage to destroy what was in your way you should be afraid of it—afterwards.'

"This was too plain for the woman's liking. It must always be a grotesque matter for two people to discuss the destruction of a third, in particular when these two affect to love each other; how reconcile the dignity of mutual love, the pain of mutual passion, and the baseness of a plot to murder?

" 'You must tell me no more,' she said, 'lest I misunderstand you. What weight do you think to put on my conscience?'

"But they understood each other very well. There was no need for her to say more than this:

" 'Susanna is not a strong woman. She may get the ague again this winter, like she had last—do you remember how she shivered, even in church that time, all her ornaments rattling? I won't pretend that I should weep for her if she should go, Philip.'

" 'There is no obligation on you nor I to wish Susanna to live.'

"The mist lifted. The ancient dark landscape was clear above them. A few sheep were cropping in the middle distance and crows flapped towards the far-off hills. There was no autumn red or gold up there, The winter came with a back decay.

"Each of them marvelled a little, as far as there was room in their hearts for marvel, how it was they had not noticed before the strangeness of the country in which they had both been brought up.

"He had travelled much, she had never left her native hills, yet to both of them came the conviction that this was an unearthly landscape.

"A shaft of sunshine like a sword struck a distant peak.

"The man looked at it and made an effort to escape his doom, though he knew it was as vain for him to try to do this as for one chained and riveted to a rock to endeavour to twist his iron fetters from the implacable granite. He said, his voice low and muffled on the rising wind:

" 'Why don't we go away, Barbara, you and I? I know so many places in far-off countries. We should be quite safe, Susanna could do nothing. We might even be married abroad by some monk, if that would satisfy you. I think of houses, white, with jasmine growing up the front, and little green balconies and two shutters, where you and I, Barbara—I can get the money, a mortgage on all the lands.'

"She said exactly the words that he was expecting.

" 'I won't do it, Philip, and you know as much. It would be shameful, a slight and a disgrace. No woman of my family has ever been degraded like that.' She added with sad disdain, both of herself and of him: 'Probably you would get tired of me, or I of you, and both of us of love itself so far away in the strangeness and the heat. Exiled.'

" 'We might tire of each other, of love itself, here,' he replied. 'Do you think that you could be content in Vavasour Hall—afterwards?'

" 'After what, Philip?'

" 'After her death and our marriage.'

"She glanced down at her feet, the damp was penetrating her thick latchet shoes.

" 'It is I who will catch an ague, Philip. I must go home, and I do not think that I will come here again. It is a melancholy, perhaps a blasted spot.'

" 'I know none other so remote,' he replied, 'and I have always thought, Barbara, that the Wishing Stone would, in the end, bring us luck.'

" 'What have you wished on it?' she asked curiously.

" 'It's part of the spell, is it not, we may not tell one another? But you know, Barbara, what I have always wished.'

" 'Yes, for us to live together always. We ought to if it was meant we should. But how? How stupid a barrier marriage can be, Philip! A few words and a ring and she is there, always.'

" ' "Until death do us part," ' he smiled, and he drew his handkerchief from his left pocket-hole and wiped from his face vapour drops which the mist had left behind. Then with his forefinger he made as if he traced words on the moist air. ' "Here lies Susanna, first wife of Philip Vavasour." Could you go past that, Barbara, every time you went to church?'

" 'Why not, Philip? It would be very natural for you to marry again if you lost Susanna. Nobody could say anything; there would be no scandal or gossip.'

" 'Everyone knows that we love each other now,' he said sullenly.

" 'But once we were married they would forget that. And if they remembered I should not care.'

" 'Then you, too, Barbara, think a good deal of those words and that ring?'

" 'I too, am a woman,' she replied, using an excuse so foolish and so pitiful that he could only smile and forbear to argue.

"They moved down the hillside together, following the course of a small waterbreak that rushed from level to level beside a rude path of stone, marked here and there by low cairns which had long ago been placed to mark the ascent to the summit of the hill.

" 'We did not wish again,' he said.

" 'You meant to, Philip?'

" 'Yes, just once more.'

" 'I think there is no need. Your destiny lies in your own hands, after all.'

"They passed no living creature in their slow descent over the wet stones, the soaked heather, save the sheep with the wet glistening on the oily wool, that scarcely moved or ceased from their laborious cropping as these two passed along, the mist gathering again behind them almost as if it drove them forward.

"They came out, at length, on to lonely fields and a lonely road, there were low stone walls and ash trees heavy with brilliant scarlet fruit. He said:

" 'She ought to realise how foolish she is to try and separate us.'

"Barbara did not answer. She had to pick her way very carefully over boulders. It was necessary for them to cross the bed of a stream. The sound of falling waters was perpetually in their ears, now nearer, now farther, now almost imperceptible, then with a powerful rush that silenced their speech.

"At the end of the watercourse they had to part and each to return to that place they were forced to name home, but which they loathed. They did not dare touch each other more than the tips of their cold wet fingers.

"Barbara still said nothing. Her spirit moved in a lethargy, she thought that she would at once sleep when she returned home. She saw herself, even while she stood there, rigid, opposite her lover, sleeping in the big tester bed in her low-ceilinged chamber. She saw the curtain a little drawn from the latticed window, and the wet grey light of sunset streaming in over her own prone figure.

"He let her go and watched her; she was soon merged into the dead colours of the landscape. He knew that if he did not free himself from his wife he would lose Barbara.

"When he returned that evening to Vavasour Hall, Susanna was, as usual, waiting for him. She was aware that he had seen Barbara, and when she looked at his face, as he flung off from his arm the wet cloak he had not worn, she knew that her doom was decided."

*　　　*　　　*

Philip Fielding laid down the manuscript, and Mrs. Fielding, who had been sitting back in her chair with her eyes closed, sat up, shivering, with a startled look like one awakened from a trance.

"Were you listening or were you asleep?" he asked.

"I was listening. I don't know quite how you could write it, Philip."

This was no mere cry of anguish. She was really bewildered as to how he had had the cold-blooded courage to put down in the shape of fiction his own interview with Angela, when they had first decided upon his wife's destruction, only of course that had not been on a Northumberland hill-side, but probably in Angela's pretty little flat....

"I don't know what you mean," said Philip Fielding wearily. "Why shouldn't I write it? It just came to me, there didn't seem to be any effort at all. Besides, I believe it to be true," he added with some petulance.

"I have no doubt it's true, Philip, and that's why I wonder how you can write it. Of course," she added listlessly, "it's you and Angela. You know you were never any good at love scenes, but I suppose you can make an effort to reproduce that one."

She had recently been amazed to admiration by his skill in deception. She peered at him now, as he sat in the radiance of the lamplight, and was more intensely surprised than she had yet been by the natural way in which he said:

"Whatever do you mean, Grace? Myself and Angela! What likeness can there be? Why, of course, all that's gone right out of my head—put away in a watertight compartment. I shouldn't be likely to draw on that for anything. I've told you so, again and again."

"The whole story is you and Angela and myself," said Mrs. Fielding contemptuously. "What else? How can you be so stupid, Philip, as to try and hoodwink me? A jealous wife who won't let go, and a woman who won't come except on the terms of marriage. Why, it's too obvious."

And he did seem discomposed, even startled.

"On my word, I never thought of it," he said. Then with an awkward if charming tenderness he added: "You see, Grace, I never thought of you as a jealous wife. You were Grace always. It didn't occur to me that this story was in any way like ours. I suppose that does seem ridiculous, but really it did not. Besides, that aspect of it, the love, I mean, between Philip and Barbara, the attraction or the passion or whatever word you give it, was not my concern, it was the crime, and, you see, the crime—well, I mean that's ridiculous! It simply doesn't touch us anywhere."

"Trying to reassure me," thought Mrs. Fielding, crouching over the fire. "He's afraid he's gone a little too far, and he's trying to put me at my ease."

"Yes, of course, that part of it is absurd," she agreed, careful not to let him see her face. "The crime, how ridiculous indeed! People don't nowadays, do they? Or only people in the slums. But I still think the scene with you and Angela——"

"You're obsessed with Angela," he interrupted with a sigh and a frown. "I wrote that blessed thing to get away from Angela, but you keep on bringing her in again."

Mrs. Fielding crossed her fingers like a lattice before her face. Her muffled voice came to him with all the expression blurred:

"Are you sorry for Susanna Vavasour, Philip? How does that part of your story go? Do you really think you can enter into the feelings of that woman, shut up with that man, knowing he was planning to murder her? You say she realised her doom when he came back that night. I suppose after that she went trying to find him out and find out how he was going to do it? Wasn't there something of a tasteless, odourless white liquid? Prussic acid? I dare say she came upon that. And he, probably, once he decided, would be quite agreeable, wouldn't he?"

"I suppose he would make an effort. He'll have to be careful not to overdo that."

"Oh yes," agreed Mrs. Fielding, still talking through her fingers. "Of course he wouldn't be quite such a fool as to suddenly cover her with caresses, and pretend he'd given up Barbara. But I suppose he'd be civil and passive. In a way, contented. He wouldn't be so worried, so distraught. He'd know it was only a question of time."

"He must have been a cold-blooded devil," said Philip Fielding with a note of uneasiness in his voice. "I can't quite get into his skin even now."

"Can't you? That's a pity!" She threw back her head and laughed. "You ought to, you know, if you're to write of it in a convincing way. You ought to quite get into his skin. I suppose you've been trying to, haven't you, when you were shut up here in the library?"

"Well, yes, I have. As you know, I think I've seen him. Those descriptions of mine aren't faked. They're just like he looked to me. Even the red hair showing through the powder, and that extraordinary design of brocade on the blue coat, the seams of the sleeves and the cuffs. Wild strawberries, I think they were, and a fruit like pomegranate or a pineapple. He was larger than life, of course, they always are. It seemed to me he was about eight feet from the ground, but I couldn't get him from below the waist. He seemed to rise on a kind of vapour. Well, when I'd got as far as that, actually visualised him, I thought I'd get into his mind. It seemed to me that it would be quite simple to just, as it were, project myself into his mind. I heard myself saying to him, 'How did you do it?' I remember," continued Philip Fielding, with rising excitement, "that here, in the evening, I had my hand on his old iron stirrup, and I thought, 'How could you do it, day after day, with her shut up here, even if you hated her, why didn't you clear out? Take the other woman whether she would or no? Take the money and clear out? She'd have gone with you if she'd seen it was the only way. How could you go on loving the woman, the other woman, I mean, if you knew she wanted you to murder your wife? After all, that wretched creature had been fond of you; was fond of you still, I suppose. Weren't you sorry for her when you saw her moving about the house, doing her miserable little bits of work, trying to interest herself in stupid futilities? The only things that women had then—not that many of them have much more now."

Philip Fielding began to walk up and down the room. His wife, still crouching by the fire, watched him. When he was in the shadows he was almost lost to her, when he came within the circle of the lamp she could see him clearly. It was obvious that he was greatly moved.

"His courage is failing him. He's shirking it," she thought. "He is sorry for me, and he's beginning to hate Angela. It's clear now that Angela knows. I wonder if he'll go on? Or if he'll repent, in time? O God, do let it be in time."

"I suppose," she said, "that's where you're stuck in your story. When it comes to getting into the murderer's mind and wondering how he could do it."

"Yes, Grace, that's it, I'm stuck there. You see, one mustn't be outside, one mustn't blame or condemn, or say how horrible, or how ghastly, or what an atrocious criminal—one has to be actually inside the man to see why he did it. There's a justification for everything, you know."

"I never heard that before. It seems to me an extraordinary thing to say. But never mind that. The question is, have you found any justification for Philip Vavasour?"

"I think I have, Grace." He paused and began turning over his papers and prints. "I think that if the woman wouldn't let go, she really deserved to die. To be destroyed, to be put out of the way."

Mrs. Fielding pushed her chair back so that she was out of the reach of the firelight and quite eclipsed in the shade.

"Oh, you do, do you?"

107

"Yes, I felt that I could get into the skin of the poor wretch. I felt that I could get his viewpoint, when he didn't feel that he was doing anything ill or horrible at all, only something necessary, like killing a noxious insect, a spider."

"Why do you say a spider, Philip?"

"Oh, I don't know, they're harmless really, aren't they, and even bring luck? But I saw one just now, running over the manuscript, and it put it in my mind."

Mrs. Fielding asked her husband if he would give her a glass of water or an orange, if he had either one or the other there. He kept both in a cupboard near the bookcase.

Neither spoke until he had poured out the water and peeled the fruit and given it to her. Then he said, as if he had himself under better control:

"I don't think we ought to talk of it any more to-night, Grace. It's the sort of thing that does get on one's nerves a little. I really shall be glad when it's over. I mean, when I've got it all down and forgotten all about it."

"Will you forget all about it, Philip? How soon I wonder?"

She drank her water and played nervously with her peeled orange. He made a pretence of gathering up his papers, but merely placed them, with nervous movements, in different untidy heaps.

"Philip Vavasour," he said suddenly, and held before her an old stained engraving.

"It's not like you," she answered. "It's a strange face, I've never seen it before."

"Good God, Grace, why should it be like me? And of course it was a strange face."

"You've seen it, then?"

He did not seem to wish to talk further on the subject. She

took the engraving from him and looked at it. The unskilful hand of the engraver had reproduced handsome, heavy features, which were, to Mrs. Fielding, for all her passionate interest, expressionless. The dress was unusually rich, and finished with meticulous care.

"It is the same man," she remarked, "as he who hangs on the stairs, is it not? The green robe with the black edging. Is he dead, that one? The faces are the same. Oh, I don't know, take it away, Philip." As she handed the engraving back to her husband she added: "There's Hugh Vavasour written underneath. Why did you change the name and give him your own?"

"I don't quite know. It's an idea that came to me. It seemed to bring us closer together."

She played a while with her peeled orange, then began to tear it apart.

"The actual murder," she asked, "have you found out how that was committed? How it was that he got away with it?"

"No, I can't find out. I've told you again and again it all seems purposely blotted out. He died quite soon afterwards himself. Poisoned himself, perhaps. Cut his throat. I don't know. It seemed clear he never married Barbara. It was just a destruction of all three of them."

"Of all three of them?" Mrs. Fielding rose abruptly, her face was livid. "You mean to say that Barbara was destroyed too?"

"Of course, she was bound to be, wasn't she? How could she have gone on living after that? I mean, I think they knew that day by the tarn that it was for all of them. They talked, of course, of being married, even of being happy, but they must have known, if they'd any reason left, that that wasn't possible. He felt bound to destroy Susanna, and Barbara felt bound to stand by and allow him to do so. And I suppose they didn't see much further than that. But they must have known that it was doom and destruction."

"What happened to Barbara?" asked Mrs. Fielding, taut and rigid by the easy chair.

"I can't find out. I don't know where she's buried or where he's buried for that matter. I shall get it if I stay here long enough."

Mrs. Fielding leant against the high back of the worn, warm armchair.

"I think I could write that part of your story for you, Philip. Barbara may have gone down to a lake, put her feet into the ripples, it would be very cold, you know; she would hesitate a little before she slid underneath the water. She would fix her eyes upon an island on which grew two or three trees. She would feel that if she could reach the island it might be sanctuary, even salvation. But it was too far off and there was no boat. Nothing much grew under the trees, save a little ground ivy, which was an unpleasant red colour—the whole landscape is terrible. In between the dark trunks of the trees there just comes a little broken light, but nothing whatever living in sight. Yes, she would hesitate quite a long time, imagining the water rising up, chilling her to her heart. I believe she might die of cold before she was suffocated. But that, of course, was the end of her. Or the end of her body, for her spirit, I suppose——"

Mrs. Fielding's voice faded away.

"You're getting overwrought, Grace," said her husband uneasily. "We ought not really to be here talking like this. It was a fool's move to come here. The influence is too strong for both of us. Now we shan't be able to get away."

He seemed to speak with genuine rage and regret.

"No," said Mrs. Fielding, "I suppose we shan't get away, for quite a long time, even if we died here. One or both of us, we should still have to stay, like they did, Susanna and Philip."

She gave a quick twitching shudder, as if she shook something from her shoulders.

"Now, I'll go to bed," she said in her normal voice. "I'm tired, really, but quite all right. Don't worry about me, Philip."

She smiled at him and left the room.

*   *   *

Mrs. Fielding was much surprised to find Mrs. Mace in her room when she entered. She knew how much the housekeeper abhorred this portion of the house, and never before had she known her enter it save in broad daylight and for a brief period, just sufficient to direct the cleaning and adjustments of the chambers.

"Why, Mrs. Mace, you here! Were you wanting to speak to me? You should have come into the library. I was only just speaking with my husband over his new book."

Mrs. Fielding was really surprised to hear how ordinary her own voice sounded. She was learning from Philip how to act perfectly a horrible part.

Mrs. Mace rose from the small chintz-covered chair she had taken by the fire. She had some knitting in her hand, and a small book which Mrs. Fielding was surprised to observe was a Bible. An old-fashioned idea this, she thought, the Holy Book to keep away the evil spirits.

"I didn't like to disturb you, ma'am, but I did feel I ought to see you. I was talking to Mrs. Hicks about it, and Mary too, and we all said——"

The woman paused, Mrs. Fielding clutched the edge of the mantelpiece.

"Yes, Mrs. Mace, you all said——"

"We all said we didn't think you ought to stay here, ma'am. Neither you nor Mr. Fielding. Especially you."

"Why especially me, Mrs. Mace?"

"Well, ma'am, if you'll forgive me saying it, you don't look at all well, and haven't been these last few days, and it's only the same old story over again." The housekeeper, who was obviously making an effort over her courage, spoke more rapidly with a touch of incoherence: "It's just as we expected, ma'am. We said that Mrs. Holmes oughtn't to have let the house, and it wasn't what you might call fair, and yet we knew you'd had warnings, and you *would* have this wing. It seems really as if it's the sort of thing people can't escape. Yet we did agree, Mrs. Hicks and her husband, too, and I, that we oughtn't to stand by and see it done."

"See what done, Mrs. Mace?"

"See this house, I don't know how to put it, ma'am, see it get hold of you. It always does get hold of them, you now, one or the other. Why, there was the governess, Mrs. Holmes's governess; I didn't tell you that. I didn't dare tell anybody. We don't like to open our mouths, and this part of the house is horrible, ma'am, horrible."

"I don't feel it, Mrs. Mace."

"No, that's the nasty part of it. You don't feel it if it's got hold of you."

Mrs. Fielding smiled.

"It's very kind of you, Mrs. Mace, I do appreciate it, and I don't suppose we shall stay here much longer, either of us. I might go any day, so might my husband. But this old story has got hold of him. It *is* only an old story, you know, and I don't think there's much of it true. He can't find out very much, and as for the ghost and the hauntings, well, all old houses have that, and I'm not susceptible, as I told you at first. I'm not likely to see anything."

"Maybe, ma'am, you're not likely to see anything." The housekeeper seemed to search anxiously in her mind for some expression to explain her fears. "It gets hold of you," was all she could repeat.

"Yes, I see what you mean, You're afraid *for* me. Perhaps, if you were a little cleverer you'd be afraid *of* me."

"Afraid of you, ma'am?" There was a note of incredulity in the housekeeper's voice. She took two steps away from where Mrs. Fielding, a tall, dark figure in the dark green dress, leant against the mantelshelf.

"Don't you think t might get into me as well as into him?"

"I didn't say it had got into him, if you mean Mr. Fielding, ma'am."

"No, but that's what you thought—the murderer you know. I know all the tales, all the explanations, the influence, the atmosphere, an evil spirit left behind finding another body to work out its purpose, its *thwarted* purpose, Mrs. Mace, don't forget that. This man Vavasour never did it."

"Never did what, ma'am."

The housekeeper fell back another pace.

"Never did the murder—how stupid everybody is! It came to me quite a long time ago, or was it only yesterday? One doesn't count the days much in a place like this. Of course it was perfectly clear. He wanted to murder her, but she discovered it in time, and she murdered him!"

"Has Mr. Fielding fount that out?" stammered the housekeeper. "Has he found that out, ma'am, among all them old papers?"

"No; he doesn't know, or pretends he doesn't know. I do, I am quite certain."

Mrs. Mace rubbed her hands nervously together and retreated still farther into the shadows by the great bed. Ever since the Fieldings had come to Medlar's Farm she had been prepared for something—outlandish—as she vaguely termed her dreadful fears; but when the terror came it was almost unendurable. Mrs. Fielding was smiling; she felt certain exhalation, as if she had stepped beyond all human woes.

"Queer that I should be the first to find the truth about her, eh, Mrs. Mace? When Barbara came over the day she found him dying and Susanna had gone out to the lake—they thought he had drowned her first, then poisoned himself, but Barbara *knew.*"

The housekeeper listened intently as Mrs. Fielding continued:

"Don't you see? I saw that statue, when she took me by the hand, showing me the devil pursuing a poor tormented wretch. He turned round suddenly and trapped his tormentor. So did she, this miserable Susanna. She wasn't going to be murdered, Mrs. Mace; she wasn't going to run away and let the other woman have him. She murdered him. She found that tasteless, odourless white essence that he'd prepared for her, that he was watching for an opportunity to give her, and she changed it, and she put it into some drink for him, and he died with that horrible swiftness that he had prepared for her. She had quite as much courage as he had, Mrs. Mace. Women have, you know. She could stand by and see him drop dead. It was better than letting him go to the other. Don't you think so too? Don't you think she was justified?"

"I never heard that part of the story," stammered the housekeeper, "but very likely it is so. I don't know. It's a long time ago, and one hears this and hears that. But all I do know, ma'am, is that you shouldn't be staying here; it's having a bad effect on you, and you're not the woman you were when you came here. It's not only I who say so

—nobody can ever live in this wing of the house. You ought to come into the old Viking part. It may be rough and rude, but it's quite wholesome."

Mrs. Fielding shook her head.

"You're mistaken. I'm quite well."

"Then there are the cottages," urged the housekeeper, as if the other woman had not spoken. "I'm sure Mrs. Hicks would do her best to make you comfortable. They'd give you a nice bedroom, and everything clean and pleasant. The children about might take your mind off things."

"What makes you think my mind is on—*things*?"

"Anyone can see it, if you'll forgive me, ma'am. You're hardly eating, and I don't think you're sleeping; taking drugs at night. Mr. Fielding has said to me many a time that he's worried about you. I felt it was my duty to speak, knowing the house as I do."

"Oh, my husband has spoken to you about me, has he?"

"Yes, ma'am, he seemed anxious, sorry he brought you here. He told me you'd be going away, and I hoped you would. Every day I hoped you'd say so."

"Well, I shall be going quite soon, Mrs. Mace. Just give me a few more days. My husband wants to get some more of his story clear."

"I don't think that story will ever be written, ma'am, if you'll forgive me. Certainly it won't ever be made into a book for people to read. Besides, if he wants to go on with it, that's no reason for you to stay, is it?"

"I've got another reason, Mrs. Mace. I think, yes, I want to stay until they submerge the church—Crompton Old Church—you know, and bring up the body of Susanna Vavasour. She said she would not rest until the Resurrection, didn't she? I'd like to see what's left of her."

"I shouldn't do that if I was you, ma'am, I really shouldn't. There won't be anything there, nothing but a few bones, nothing to explain the mystery. I don't suppose they'd let anyone in. Anyhow, it's all going to be done private, and late at night."

"They couldn't keep me away," said Mrs. Fielding, "if I made up my mind to be there."

"Well, now, ma'am, don't those kind of wishes and fancies show you're not yourself? You've been used to a different life. London, and lots of people—going about. This is no place for you to come to."

"I wonder why you're so concerned about me, Mrs. Mace. Do you see me marked down as a kind of victim? Like those trees in the forest that have the cross on them? They're the ones that are going to get the axe, are they not?"

Mrs. Mace stood silent a second, thoughtfully and anxiously eyeing through her thick pebble glasses the other woman. When she spoke, it was in a changed tone.

"Well, I shouldn't think any more of it to-night, ma'am. I should go to bed if I was you, and let me bring you a nice cup of hot milk or tea or whatever you fancy, and you'd better take one of your sleeping draughts. You don't look to me as if you were going to get a wink."

"Very well, Mrs. Mace." Mrs. Fielding sank into the easy chair in which the housekeeper had kept her vigil. "I'll go to bed, and I'll try to go to sleep. There's to-morrow and the day after, and I dare say one or two days after that. It's not all quite clear to me yet," she added in a musing tone.

Mrs. Mace began to prepare the bed.

"She made an appeal to Barbara, of course. I can see her going over the mountains. Begged Barbara to do as she had threatened, marry another man and go right away. She thought to herself, 'If Barbara does that, of course he will not have any reason to destroy me. He won't do it, and we might, in time, come together again. The enchantment might be broken. But Barbara won't go away.' "

She turned and looked at the housekeeper over her shoulder.

"Don't you see, Mrs. Mace, that put all the responsibility on to Barbara? She would not go away, and Susanna Vavasour was cornered. Barbara would not go away, and he was just waiting for a chance to murder her, so she—why, it's like the toad, isn't it?"

"The toad, ma'am?" There's no such things here, I assure you.

"The toad in the story; it was cornered and started and stared at the man who was trying to gaze it to death, until the man died."

"That's a horrid fancy, ma'am, I must say," said the housekeeper in great uneasiness. "You've got your head all full of the wrong sort of tales. I dare say," she added in a non-committal tone, "it was Mrs. Vavasour who murdered her husband. I always heard they died, one after the other, here together. But where he's buried I never heard any say."

"Perhaps," smiled Mrs. Fielding, dropping her graceful head on her thin hands, "she contrived to make it look like suicide, and he was buried at the crossroads, with a stake through him? No, that wouldn't be right, because he walks, doesn't he, in a blue coat? And suicides never walk."

"I'm not so sure of that," replied Mrs. Mace, reluctantly fascinated by this forbidden topic, like one drawn against her will into a magic circle. "I think some do—you haven't *seen* anything, have you, ma'am?"

"No—I've just imagined things."

"I've heard other people who have been here say that, ma'am. I've often wondered what this imagining is—that poor young governess now———"

"Did she see anything? What happened to her?"

Mrs. Mace pursed her lips, afraid of having already said too much. She was being drawn into that dreadful discussion that she most desired to avoid. But the next question that Mrs. Fielding asked startled the housekeeper beyond discretion.

"Do you know if it is easy to get hold of cyanide of potassium, Mrs. Mace?"

"Whatever makes you ask that, ma'am? Why, that's the name the doctor said——" She checked herself too late.

"What doctor? When? Cyanide of potassium—who got some? It's instant death, you know."

"It was the governess, ma'am. She did get some—she told the chemist that it was to destroy an old dog——"

"But she took it herself, I suppose, Mrs. Mace? Or did she give it to someone else?"

"Oh no, ma'am, nothing of the kind! Only it was found out that she had got it, I mean—and there was trouble."

"A likely story," smiled Mrs. Fielding indifferently.

The housekeeper resolved to say no more on the matter. She took a long time adjusting the bed, arranging the reading lamp, and placing the hot-water bottle between the sheets, and as she went about her tasks she glanced frequently and apprehensively at the woman drooping in the chair by the fire.

Mrs. Fielding spoke no more. When the housekeeper at length approached her and asked her if she should assist her to undress and get to bed, she found that the tall, dark, elegant woman was asleep, her head still clasped in her hands and her elbow on the chair. Mrs. Mace, her rather hard-featured face set in lines of agitated resolution, stared at the sleeping woman for a while. Mrs. Fielding stirred. Her elbow sunk from the chair, her hand fell and her head drooped forward. She muttered: "I'll do it to-morrow."

The housekeeper gently laid her back on the cushions, so that in that natural attitude she continued her slumber. Then, with a precise gesture, she placed the Bible on the sleeping woman's knees.

"Never say, 'I'll do it to-morrow' unless ye add 'if the Lord permits,' " she murmured. For she was a woman who found religion a strong consolation in many troubles and bereavements, and texts were more often in her mind than on her tongue.

When she had assured herself that Mrs. Fielding was deep in her exhausted sleep, the housekeeper took up the small lamp from the table by the bed and began to very cautiously and systematically search the room, every corner of which was familiar to her. She did this in as noiseless a manner as possibly, and continually paused to glance at the sleeping figure by the fire. Mrs. Fielding stirred, groaned, and once more repeated she "would do it to-morrow," but remained unconscious of the activities of the housekeeper, which included a close inspection of the small medicine cupboard in the corner. She examined carefully every object that she found there. None of them was calculated to arouse suspicion, for they were all known to her, or else, by reason of their colour, substance, or smell, obviously not what she sought.

It did not occur to her to inspect the contents of the atomiser of pink glass painted with blue flowerets that stood on the top of the shelf.

She stood thoughtful, not wholly satisfied.

"They get so cunning. I ought to speak to her husband. I wonder why they came here? She seems to me the last sort of person—and what made her mention that horrid stuff?"

Mrs. Mace hesitated. She would have liked to put Mrs. Fielding to bed, but dared not rouse her from what seemed a deep sleep, likely to last till morning. And then, as she became aware of the steady silence and of where she was, a place she had avoided during the whole of her stay at Medlar's Farm, and avoided especially at this hour, there was something else that she dare not do, and that was remain any longer in this solitary chamber.

She made Mrs. Fielding as comfortable as possible in the easy chair, and then, with hesitation, as if she was doing a mean action, she took the Bible from the sleeping woman's knee. She had not the courage to traverse the Georgian wing of Medlar's Farm, at this hour of the night, without the Holy Book under her arm.

*   *   *

Mrs. Fielding woke suddenly, instantly alert, and instantly aware that this was the depth of the night in which she was sunk as one might be sunk in the depth of a lake—away from all humanity.

The fire had sunk to a heap of ash, the lamp was still burning. She took this up and went directly to the library with as little hesitation as if some potent presence beckoned her onwards.

Her husband's papers, books, prints, lay in disorder close to the reading lamp. She lit this and put her own smaller light beside it, so that the table, encumbered with odd objects, was fully illuminated. There was the rusty spur and the shrivelled mitten of tarnished thread side by side; there was the print of Hugh Vavasour in his elaborate brocade coat, and there were the old books, musty, worm-holed, foxed, with rubbed leather covers and long letters in sepia-coloured ink that held the obscure and incomplete records of his tragedy.

Mrs. Fielding seated herself in the large chair her husband used, and then paused in her movements in order to listen to the stillness that held the large dark crowded room like a spell.

Then she began running over the books, the spent husks of dead thoughts, passions, and pleasures. She looked sullenly at the headpieces and finials, queer symbolic devices of monsters, masonic signs, the arcana of the Rosy Cross, and none of them meant anything to her save the repetition of the word *Finis*, which she came frequently upon when turning these dry pages and became multiplied before her eyes until it was written all over the dark air beyond the circle of the lamplight.

"There is no need for Philip to read me any more of his story, I know it quite well—I could write some of it myself——"

She drew a sheet of paper towards her, and began to write as if she was taking down a dictation.

*   *   *

"Barbara could wait no longer. He had so frequently given her to understand that it would be soon now—that they would be immediately free. Nothing had been put plainly in words between them, but he knew what she expected. The suspense was exhausting her; she frequently made herself possets of borage and hellebore to keep off melancholy, and her sick looks were remarked by her father, who chid her harshly for her misplaced passion.

"So, this autumn day she came alone, on foot, to Vavasour Hall. She knew that he had had the poison long in the house. He had procured it from an apothecary in Newcastle. Why did he hesitate? She was in the mood to strangle the narrow-faced, railing wife with her own hands. It was a day of wind and of low clouds scudding before the wind; the sheep stood with their backs to it, and the long grey wool was blown over their imbecile faces. Barbara walked rapidly, brittle fragments of fern and heather clung to her skirt, and her flesh became cold from the bitter air. When she reached Vavasour Hall there was no one about. The gates stood wide; the gardener's tools lay on the lawn which was strewn with dead leaves like withered garlands, but there was no gardener. The bleak light that fitfully penetrated the quick-driven clouds lay along the avenue of elms that had been in shade a few days ago. But a great storm had stripped off the last of the harsh, crinkled yellow leaves, and the black twigs showed bare against the lurid, vaporous heavens. The doors and windows of Vavsour Hall all stood open despite the wind; some of the curtains were blown out against the grey stonework. Barbara caught her cloak which, filled with wind, seemed to pull her back, and entered the open, vacant doorway.

"There was no one within. He had done it, then. Some calamity had struck the household into silence. No doubt in the large funeral chamber the women were already laying out their mistress in the state bed with the black plumes where none but the dead ever slept. The crimped cap would be drawn round the narrow chin, the greedy hands folded on the barren breast, and the shroud folded and tied over the despised body that had been violently destroyed.

" 'It would be wiser for me to go,' thought Barbara, but she remained rigid in the empty hall, the wind, tearing up the bare avenue and in at the open door, disordering her hair and her garments.

"Here, to this house, she would come as a bride; in the nuptial chamber where he had so often slept with Susanna, she, the second wife, would take off her bridal garters in the dark and toss them, through the half-open door, to the waiting maids in the anteroom. Already, in secret, she had embroidered those garters, ribbons of yellow, violet, and blue. Here in this house she would wake, after her marriage night, and see her husband beside her, and they would look at each other in the horrid bleached light of dawn and wonder if they heard a foot without or a scratching on the panel. Or would they, that night, sleep at all? Would they not rather lie wakeful, cold, and apart?

"She faced the wind, turning to leave the silent house when she heard a cry falling down the dark stairs: 'Barbara!'

"She obeyed this summons and went upstairs, passing no one on her way; but every door and window was set wide as if something had rushed through the house, striving to escape by every opening.

"She heard her name again, nearer now; it was his voice, though much changed. She traced it to the great chamber that had been in her mind when she waited below; the sleeping chamber of the master of the house, where so many Vavasours had been born and had died. Barbara crept in, cold from the constant wind and her constant fear.

"He was on the floor beside the monstrous bed; he had dragged down the sheets and coverlets in some frantic clutch; his shirt was torn aside, his neck and chest bare as if for torture or decapitation, and his red hair hung loose like the untidy mane of a bull. Barbara, in an instant fury, began to mock at this overthrow; what was this man to her then but a weapon broken in the hand?

" 'Oh, coward! Is this your strength of purpose? Do you want to betray us?'

" 'Is that you, Barbara? I cannot see.'

" 'It is I. Were you not calling on me?'

" 'Maybe. I am in some pain and think on the cause of it.'

"His voice was thick and his great eyes were dull; like a powerful, half-slaughtered animal he heaved his length by the bed and gnawed at his fingers. The rain broke suddenly from the clouds and hurled long spears of water into the room which was drenched in a pale storm light.

" 'Is this remorse?' asked Barbara bitterly.

"He began to cry, like a child—yet his tears were the difficult tears of the dying.

" 'She found the drug—and gave it to me—I waited too long.'

" 'Ah! Where is she?'

" 'Gone. Gone. Gone. To the lake——' ' "

*　　　*　　　*

Mrs. Fielding came downstairs very late the next morning; she was angry with herself for oversleeping, and confused as to what had happened the night before. She remembered falling asleep in the library, then waking just as it was beginning to get light, and going upstairs again with the little low-flickering lamp in her hand, then falling, dressed, on her bed, and sleeping— without a sedative that time. The oblivion at which she had snatched greedily had been delicious, but it was hideously vexatious that she should have been late, for as she crept into the Tudor room, walking very softly, she surprised her husband reading a letter from Angela. She saw at once on the notepaper the name of the hotel she had visited and Angels'a contemptuously individual handwriting.

Philip Fielding started when he realised that his wife was standing beside him, and deliberately, with an almost childish movement, hid the letter. She had seen two words written in that large hand, one was her own name "Grace," and the other was "poison."

"You might let me read that, Philip."

"I can't. I didn't mean you to know it had come. Angela ought not to have written. She said she wouldn't. You mustn't think she means anything, Grace."

"Show it to me, then."

"I can't."

He folded the letter up and put it in an inner pocket of his coat.

"You'll have to trust me to that extent, Grace. Sit down and take your breakfast. Mrs. Mace is worried about you. Thinks you're not too well, that the house is really affecting you. I must arrange for you to go away."

She took her seat at the breakfast-table and eyed his breast where, under the tweed coat, lay Angela's letter, with the two words, her own name and "poison." Angela was being very daring. Wouldn't that letter be evidence—afterwards? But of course he would destroy it.

She made another effort to goad him, not because she hoped to see the letter, but because she wanted to inflict torture on him, as he had inflicted torture on her. "Let me read it. Why shouldn't I? I told you Angela and I were quite frank one with another. There oughtn't to be any secrets now."

"Grace, this isn't what you think it is. It's something between Angela and myself. It's nothing to do with—with—any feeling we have one for another. But I can't let you read the letter. It's most unfortunate you should have seen it. I shall destroy it at once. Don't think it's the kind of letter one treasures."

"I suppose not," smiled Mrs. Fielding.

He abruptly left the breakfast-table. She remained in her place, but neither ate not drank that morning. She thought:

"Angela is urging him to do something. But I suppose by now he's found out that the poison's no use. That must worry him. But, of course, the last thing he'd think of is that I'd changed it. I expect he believes that whoever gave it him, fooled him. No doubt he's already decided on something else. A knife, or a rope? I expect he'll suggest taking me out—a long expedition, insist on telling Mrs. Mace that I'm going away soon."

She nodded across the breakfast-table. She thought that at the other side of the white cloth and the handsome, antique silver, there sat another woman in a dark green dress, with a handful of pale hair fine as floss silk, her companion and her guide, who looked at her, nodded and said, "Now."

She tried to remember what had happened last night, but she was no longer capable of a coherent thought. She frowned, trying to recall what the young man in the old-fashioned chemist's shop had said to her—"Cyanide of potassium—a deadly poison," and then he had handed back to her the little bottle that contained the liquid that she afterwards transferred to the atomiser of pink glass.

Transferred with what intention?

If Philip had said that the damp had touched his throat—she might say—"This is a very good lotion I had made up in town, try it with the spray." Or was not that part of her dreams, that, on waking, she never could recapture?

Last night, surely, Susanna Vavasour had come to her and told

126

her exactly how it was done. But that was part of what she could not remember.

She went into the library where her husband seemed to be clearing up the materials for his work.

"I wrote some of your story last night, Philip; did you find it?"

"I? No—nothing."

Distressed, she began to search among the papers.

"Oh, I am sure I wrote—pages. This house, standing empty, and the wind blowing through——"

He took her hands to stay her restless searching.

"Grace, you are getting full of fancies, really. There was nothing here when I came down this morning, but a pile of blank paper, like I left last night——"

She averted her glance as she reflected, cunningly: "Of course he is still trying to deceive me. He must have been rather frightened when he read what I had written and realised that I *knew*, so he destroyed the sheets."

"Grace, I am giving it up, and the house. It was all an awful mistake. It hasn't come out a bit like I thought it would."

"No?"

"No." He was still holding her hands. "There is no escape here. We must get away. I can't bear that you should feel that this horrible old story is like ours——"

"I suppose not."

"Of course—it couldn't be. I don't believe these Vavasours ever existed. They are phantoms. Monsters. They have nothing to do with us."

"I suppose not."

"Grace, you look so lifeless. What is it, dear?"

He put his arms round her and she lay against his breast thinking the while of Angela's letter in which was the word "poison" between her and his heart.

"We were happy once, weren't we? How could you let it happen?"

She began to weep in her utter woe. He comforted her in a low voice and she slipped away from him. She believed that she saw a restless shape that moved to and fro whispering the word "Now."

"I'll go upstairs, Philip, and lie down till luncheon."

*   *   *

When Mrs. Fielding went upstairs she cautiously entered her husband's room and looked into his dispatch case. The little bottle labelled "Headache Drops" that she had filled with water was gone.

Upon this discovery she went to the corner cupboard in her room and took down the pink glass atomiser. There was about an inch of liquid at the bottom. Would it be enough? Had she lost some in the transference from one vessel to another?

She found the original bottle she had used, and very carefully poured into this the contents of the atomiser. Enough, surely. But she wished that she could more clearly remember what the chemist has told her—that, like so much that lay stagnant in her mind, was hard to recall.

She put the bottle in her handbag. Cornered, like the toad, like the mouse, like Susanna Vavasour.

As she came listlessly down the stairs, with this in her handbag, her husband met her by the newel-post, and affectionately took her arm.

"Listen, Grace. I'm not going to have any more of this nonsense. Mrs. Mace is right. You don't look at all fit. I'm going to send you away. I've made all the arrangements. If you'd rather, I'll take you away, the day after to-morrow. Let's make it Italy, after all. You can be ready, can't you? Get all you want together in a little while?"

"All I want?" thought Mrs. Fielding. "What is he thinking of? A shroud, a spade, quicklime?"

She allowed him to take her into the Tudor room. The luncheon was ready. He was very agreeable during the meal, and watched her anxiously: "Wondering why I don't drop and die, wondering why he can't destroy me."

They quietly talked of their coming departure from Medlar's Farm and discussed where they should go in Italy.

Mrs. Mace brought in the coffee, and set it on a tray of pierced silver by a bowl of pretty pink, waxy flowers which had just been sent in from the greenhouses; they seemed to Mrs. Fielding to be the same kind of blooms as those she had seen hanging in the wire basket while she talked with Angela; while she gave Angela her last chance.

"Philip and I have very few more words to say to one another, and I suppose those few will be absolutely trivial and futile. We got as near to the truth as we could, but now we seem to have receded again. There's nothing more to be said, only something to be done."

The kindness of his manner strengthened her purpose, for it confirmed her conviction of his callous cruelty. He was soothing her, luring her on. She began to turn over in her mind what the moment, which she intended to forestall, might be like? When would his manner change? Would he, still with a caress, leap on her? Would he, drawing her to him, as if to kiss her, close his fingers round her throat? She had often read, as a child, with horror of murders. Particularly murders in lonely places. She remembered an old cut of a gig blowing along a solitary road and one of the two occupants turning to shoot the other,[10] and she had often thought, even then, "What was the last friendly word? Did one begin to

10 Cut: woodcut print.

look sullen, the other frightened, or was there just a laugh, and then a flash? There must have been one awful second when the victim saw the murderer drawing out his weapon, when he realised—'that moment is for me.' "

"It's a glorious day, not a scrap of mist for once, nor a drop of rain. I think we might take a long drive this afternoon."

"So he can't wait any longer."

"I should like," he said, "a long drive—to get quite away—wouldn't you?"

"Oh, Philip, there's a large spider over there. Do move it."

While his back was turned, while he searched for the insect, she had taken the bottle out of her bag and emptied the contents into his cup of coffee.

Philip Fielding returned to her side.

"I didn't see any spider."

"Oh, I suppose it ran away. Your coffee is getting cold."

She watched him drink, which he did without comment.

*   *   *

As Mrs. Fielding passed down the road on her way to the lake she saw a gleaming blue sports car pass in between the stone piers of the gates to Medlar's Farm.

Angela, who could not keep away; Angela, who would now watch him die, as Susanna Vavasour had watched her lover die.

Mrs. Fielding nodded and smiled to the pale-haired woman in the dark green dress who was her constant companion, and walked on with more eager steps towards her inevitable destination.

*   *   *

When Mrs. Mace opened the door to Angela, she thought:

"So here you are again, my lady. You're the cause of all the trouble, I'll be bound."

"I'll just leave the car there. I shan't be a moment. Is Mrs. Fielding in the house?"

"I think so, ma'am. I believe she's upstairs in her room. I'll go and see. Mr. Fielding is in the library."

"I won't disturb him. It's Mrs. Fielding I want to see. If she's out I'll wait."

Angela's manner was downcast and troubled; Mrs. Mace's instinctive dislike of her quietened.

"Will you come in, miss, and wait in the Tudor room? I think that's the most cheerful."

To this strange remark Angela replied:

"I think the whole house is horrible. I'd rather stay in the hall until you know if Mrs. Fielding is in or not." She added impulsively: "This is a ghastly place, so lonely. As I drove along I saw two or three hearses. You know, it seems like a nightmare, not real—hearses on that lonely road."

For a moment Mrs. Mace was herself startled, and then she smiled.

"Oh yes, it was to be to-day, of course, if they couldn't finish last night. Those aren't really what you can call hearses, miss."

"Oh, I'm sure they were."

"Well, they're going to take the bones out of Crompton Old Church. The church isn't going to be drowned for a few weeks yet, but they're beginning to take the bones away, to the big cemetery at Hexham, I think. They haven't been burying there for a long time, so it can only be people who've been dead for years."

"I suppose that does make it better. Still, it was a nasty sight."

131

As she spoke Philip Fielding came down the wide dark stairs. As soon as she saw him and before he could speak she cried out awkwardly and rapidly:

"Oh, Phil! I want to see Grace—rather badly."

"I think she's upstairs."

"I'm just going to see, sir." And Mrs. Mace left them together, not without a shrewd backward glance.

"Come into the library," said Philip Fielding, and Angela followed him with apprehension and reluctance in her look and movement.

As soon as the door had closed behind them she began at once:

"Look here, Phil, you'll think I'm a beast to be here again, but it really *is* to see Grace."

"Mrs. Mace has gone up to find her. I think she's in her room. But what do you want to see Grace for, Angela? She came over to see you the other day, didn't she?"

"Yes, she did. I don't suppose she told you what it was all about."

"No, she didn't. I guessed a little."

"Of course it's all getting hateful to you, as it is to me," said Angela rapidly, twisting her fingers together. "She came and asked me to give up, go right away, like I said I would before, and I just told her 'No!' said I couldn't, but I've been thinking it over, Phil, and I've decided that she's right."

"You are really going away, Angela?"

"Yes, I am. Far away. I can still get a tour, Canada, Africa; oh, I don't know where. I'll try to find another man too," she laughed defiantly. "There's no cure for one love affair but another, is there?"

He did not answer, but stood rigid before the pile of papers on which his finger-tips rested.

"You see," said Angela, "I stood firm while she was there, I didn't want to make any pretences. I was trying to be frank, but after she'd gone, I thought it over. She scared me, Phil, she really did. She said that if I didn't give up, something dreadful would happen, that it was the last chance. And, you know, I've been thinking it over, and it did seem to me that we were on the verge of something dreadful, and that it wasn't worth while."

"What wasn't worth while, Angela?"

"Well, you and I. I don't say I'm through with it—I care awfully, but somehow——"

"You've seen Grace's point of view?"

"Well, I always saw that—I don't know, I don't want to talk about it. Of course we made a mistake," with a certain violent contempt. "We ought to have had the usual sly intrigue. That was the old-fashioned way, and those people knew what they were doing. This being frank, telling the truth from the first, and talking about divorce, and being so candid and so respectable, you see what it ends in. I don't like the look of Grace," she repeated.

"You're right that she's not been well here. I ought to have noticed it. I came here on—I don't quite know what with—when we—when you gave me up—I thought I'd come here and throw myself into the history of the place—you know I've tried that trick before, evoking the past, and getting into the skins of dead people, and Grace was always the kind that didn't mind a bit—anything odd, or occult, I mean, and I really thought the peace and quiet would be good for her." He hurried on painfully with his explanations, not looking at Angela, who was leaning against one of the high book-cases. "She seemed all right at first, and I did get absorbed."

"Into forgetting me?" interrupted Angela.

"Well, even into that. Yes, I must say you got blotted out a little. The influence of the place," he glanced round the dark room, "is very powerful."

"I always thought it was pretty ghastly. I don't know how you could live here."

"I had to do something violent and unusual. I had to get right away and make a clean cut, or I couldn't have borne it. I believe I've done it—made the clean cut."

"You mean you believe you can manage without me?"

"I think so, Angela."

"You beast," she said on a sigh. "But it's better. I dare say I can do it too. One doesn't want to be utterly loathsome. You ought to feel very flattered. Of course you understand that it isn't that Grace is so much—crazy about you. It's all you stood for—all she put into the concern as it were that you knocked sky-high."

"Yes, I understand. I dare say I can make it up to her. We shall get along somehow. And you're right to be scared. I'm going to take her away to Italy. I think that's best. Mrs. Mace, that's the housekeeper here, spoke to me this morning—said she was quite strange, poor Grace, last night. Perhaps the house is getting hold of her."

"Strange, in what way?" asked Angela sharply.

"Oh, I don't know, she was talking about the old story. She's been visiting the churchyard where the woman was buried who used to live here. It's an old murder tale, rather sickening, no doubt. A story of jealousy."

"How on earth could you bring Grace where there's a story of jealousy and murder?"

"I suppose I was a fool. You know, it never occurred to me till she spoke the other night. She said when I was reading out some of my stuff—'Why, that's our story!' "

Angela did not answer; her huddled attitude showed a weight of uneasiness.

"She's a long time coming down," said Philip Fielding with a touch of concern. "I suppose Mrs. Mace can't find her. We were warned not to go into that Georgian wing of the house, it's supposed to be haunted. It's nonsense, of course, in a way, yet I don't know. I thought of buying the place, of probing the whole thing to the bottom."

"I don't know anything about it, but it seems to me the kind of thing you can't probe to the bottom, that will get hold of you and do for you, but that you'll never understand. Cut free, Phil, leave it alone, clear out, don't buy it."

"I don't mean to, not now. What are you going to say to her, Angela? Do you really want to see her?"

"Did you show her my letter? You must have got it this morning."

"No, how could I? It had got that bit in it—about—that rubbish about the poison, you know. I couldn't show her that. You should have written more carefully——"

"I wasn't thinking of being careful. She frightened me. I thought, when I came to think it over, that she might mean to poison herself——"

"I don't know why—and you shouldn't have written it."

Angela Campion ignored this tone of irritated rebuke, though it came oddly from one who had hitherto always spoken to her with love and deference; she defended herself.

"I had to warn you."

"But I couldn't show her the letter, don't you see? And that hurt her—and I can't see what made you think of poison—she couldn't get any here."

"I thought of it because I nearly got to that point myself," said Angela sullenly. "I was looking round for something, after you'd said good-bye."

"I've not forgotten. But it was only a wild threat."

"You were scared, though, weren't you? Don't you remember that you took away that bottle of headache drops you found inside my cigarette-box?"

"Yes, I came upon them yesterday in my case and threw them away. What has that got to do with it?"

"Well, that stuff was harmless, just something for neuralgia— but I had something in the flat that wasn't——"

"What do you mean, Angela?"

"I got it in Paris. Quite easy. I didn't take it, I don't mean to— but I came near enough to it to realise that Grace might—that's why I wrote, that's why I'm over here to-day. She did threaten something dreadful."

The housekeeper entered after a knock that neither of them had heard.

"Mrs. Fielding doesn't seem to be in the house, sir. Hicks and Mrs. Hicks—Mary—they've none of them seen her in the garden or the grounds. She hasn't ordered the car. She must have gone for a walk."

"Well," said Philip Fielding, with something of an effort, "I suppose that's quite natural and reasonable, isn't it, Mrs. Mace?"

"The walk in itself's quite natural and reasonable, sir, but if I was you I'd be inclined to go after Mrs. Fielding, because I don't think she's in a very natural or reasonable humour."

Mrs. Mace repeated her account of the agitation and strange behaviour of Grace Fielding on the evening before; and she added some details which she had not thought necessary to give before, for she was alarmed by the appearance of Angela and by the disappearance of Mrs. Fielding.

"You see, sir, I've been there before. I didn't like the look of any of it, and I made a good search of the room before I left her."

"A search of the room? What were you looking for, Mrs. Mace?"

"For a revolver, sir, or a knife, or anything that you might do a mischief with."

"You had the same thought that I had!" exclaimed Angela. "You see, Phil, I was right."

"Say exactly what you mean, Mrs. Mace."

"I thought she might do something horrid, sir. You'll take my meaning. I've been there before. It was one of the young governesses, and then a lady that stayed here. Only just in time we was then, and with Miss Bates—too late. You see, sir, it's the influence of the place. It gets hold of somebody; it doesn't seem to have got hold of you, but it's got hold of her."

"You didn't find anything?"

"No, sir." Mrs. Mace hesitated a moment; no doubt it was all nonsense and just her nervousness, and no need to make a fuss. So she said: "No, sir, nothing at all." Yet could not resist adding: "But I don't like the look of it. They get so clever. Poor Miss Bates, now, she had it hidden away. Cyanide of potassium the doctor said it was——"

"I'll go after her," interrupted Philip Fielding as if he had not heard this. "I'll find her at once."

"I wish you would, sir," said Mrs. Mace. "You see," she repeated again, "I've been there before."

"I'll come too," said Angela. "The Bluebird will take us anywhere in no time. But what direction did she go?"

"Hicks says, miss, that she might be going to that lake where she made the car stop the other day when she went to see you. He says he didn't like the look of the way she was standing there between the trees staring down at the water. She's been up to that old churchyard, you see, sir." added the housekeeper, "and seen the old carving what they call 'The Devil Snar'd,' and she talks of that too often for my liking. There's a lot of people tried to snare the devil in this house, but none of them done it nor ever will, as I can see."

"It's the devil in ourselves we've got to snare, it seems to me," said Angela bitterly.

"That's enough for most of us," agreed Mrs. Mace.

"Shall we try the lake?" asked Philip Fielding. "I don't like to think of it. Of course it's all right. She has just gone for a walk."

"let's try it," said Angela. "She'll be all right—if I can just speak to her."

*   *   *

As the sports car sped along the lonely road Angela, rigid at the wheel and staring ahead of her, said:

"We'd better say good-bye now, Phil."

He muttered from behind his upturned collar:

"Suppose we don't find her."

"Then it will be more than ever good-bye, won't it?"

"You mean that I shall feel like a murderer?"

"O my God, Phil, don't use that word! I wish I had given way before."

He did not answer.

The clear poignant sunshine of the day was gathering into the light vapour of a fair afternoon as they reached the little wood where Mrs. Mace and Hicks, the chauffeur, had thought Mrs. Fielding might be. Beyond they could see the lake, the island, the swan.

One of the hearses going from Hexham to Crompton Old Church was standing at the verge of the close trees; the heavy black shape looked ugly in the pale glow of the pure air.

"Perhaps," murmured Philip Fielding, who could not clear his mind of phantoms, "they've got the bones of Susanna Vavasour in there."

"Who's she?" asked Angela in frightened anger, "I believe you're crazy too, Philip."

The men in charge of the hearse and two woodmen were standing at the edge of the trees. Angela stopped the blue car. She peered over the wheel.

"I think there has been an accident. I feel sick. Go and see, Phil."

"I can't. What is it? Can't you see?"

"Two of them are wet. They've got something on the grass. The same colour—a dark green dress?"

"Oh no!" cried Philip Fielding violently. They looked at each other with bitter accusation. "You are a little beast, after all." he muttered. "Why didn't you come over sooner to tell her you were clearing out?"

"You don't know what you're saying," she whimpered. "Get out and see what has happened——"

"I can't. I feel as if I'd got to the end of the world——"

One of the woodmen was coming towards the car. Angela sprang out and ran towards him; she was talking incoherently.

Grace Fielding had been in the lake half an hour. One of the woodmen had seen her slip in, but it had been a while before he could find a boat and fetch her. She had been held up by a patch of reeds and alder bushes. He had shouted for his mate and between them they had carried her to the edge of the wood. They had stopped the first vehicle that had passed—it was the hearse going to Crompton Old Church to fetch the bones of Susanna Vavasour that had been exhumed that morning.

Angela leant against one of the trees. A clean white handkerchief covered the face at her feet, which rested on trails of ground ivy. Hadn't she and Philip often wished that Grace were dead? Was that what had brought a curse on all of them?

There was no room for Mrs. Fielding in the sports car, so they laid her in the dark carriage intended for another who had tried to reach the island with the three trees.

Philip Fielding was persuaded to get out of the car and walk up and down, supported either side by the strange men. He seemed to have lost the use of his limbs, for he dragged in the friendly grip like a paralytic.

He did not know that Angela was there; she was entirely effaced from his consciousness.

His mind was focused on Medlar's Farm, where a jealous woman in a dark green dress was restlessly walking up and down, in and out, searching for another companion. He thought that he could now understand what Susanna Vavasour had done, but he fumbled round the question as to what means she had employed. When he at length said, with a chuckle at his own cleverness: "Of course, Vavasour wasn't a murderer, after all, I always knew that—it was she—it was she once he cornered her—what did Grace say about a toad?"—they thought that the shock had unsettled his mind.

A sharp, angry cry came from the fields the other side of the road. One of the woodmen said:

"It's that fool of a boy, hurt his fingers setting rabbit traps——"

Angela looked stupidly down at her bare hands as if she expected to see them bleed, while the man in worn black said to Philip Fielding:

"I suppose, sir, I'd better go to Medlar's Farm?"

*   *   *

140

"Our Phantasie... intrudes a thousand fears, suspicions, chimeras on us... so many things are offensive to us, not of themselves, but out of our corrupt judgement, jealousie, suspicion, and the like; we pull these mischiefs on our own heads."

DEMOCRITUS JUNIOR: *The Anatomy of Melancholy.*